D0897845

NIGHTMARE

NIGHTMARE

BY CHAD NICHOLAS

eBook: 978-1-7344416-2-8
Paperback: 978-1-7344416-0-4
Hardback: 978-1-7344416-4-2

Cover Art by MiblArt
Edited by Eliza Dee of Clio Editing
Formatting by MiblArt

This book is dedicated to the real Dakota.
You were the best dog ever.

"Are you watching closely?"

— *Alfred Borden*

Prologue

It was hard to breathe inside the grave. The cold touch of the soil surrounded him like a casket, numbing his body as he lay there motionless. Suddenly, he regained consciousness. He tried to breathe, but instead dirt poured into his mouth, gagging him. He opened his eyes, only to see complete and utter darkness. The ground above crashed down on him, causing his bones to crack under the weight.

He tried to fight his way upwards, but with every inch he gained, he could feel himself slipping back into unconsciousness. His lungs began collapsing, causing his chest to burn as if it was filled with hot embers. He could taste the rough, freezing dirt as it poured down into his throat, choking him. Still, he continued to crawl his way upwards, inch by inch.

Finally, he felt the dirt part above him, the chill breeze hitting his hand as it emerged from the dirt. He summoned what little strength he had left to pull himself up out of the ground.

He rolled over, coughing up the dirt. His lungs gasped for oxygen, his body shaking from the unforgiving chill of the night air. His eyes were still blurry from the dark, but he tried

to see where he was. Finally, once the blurriness subsided, he could make out the moon above him, shining down on the tombstones around him. He struggled to find his footing, trying to stand. Once he did, he looked around the cemetery in confusion.

"Where am I?" he whispered to himself. The cemetery was quiet, with only the sound of his breathing cutting through the silence. He looked around at the tombstones, which seemed to stretch out for miles. Suddenly, the cemetery became dark as the moon passed behind an old oak tree. Its branches twisted, distorting the remaining moonlight that passed through them as it shone onto the cemetery.

Suddenly the flapping of a bird's wings tore through the silence. The man jumped in his skin in fear as he searched the sky for it. His breathing quickened as he desperately tried to find it in the darkness. Finally he spotted it, resting on a tombstone in the distance. The man stepped back in horror as he made out the bird's features. Its coarse black feathers were haggard, and its talons seemed like knives in the moonlight. Its head sat slightly askew, as if it was somehow disconnected from its body. It was a crow.

The man stared at the crow as his fear turned to dread. "No, you can't be here," he whispered to himself. "You're just—" He stopped midsentence as the realization hit him. "No, no, no," he begged as his legs buckled under him and he collapsed to the ground. The fear had completely left him now as he leaned himself on a tombstone. Loneliness cascaded over him as tears streamed down his face. "Please, no," he continued to plead, knowing that it would make no difference.

As he leaned on the tombstone, staring out into the empty cemetery, he heard a horrific sound.

Sccrrreeee

It sounded as if a sawblade was being scraped across wood. The sound kept repeating. As he searched for its origin, he once again saw the crow, but it no longer perched upon the tombstone. It now rested upon a branch of the oak tree, scraping its talons against the wood. The scraping echoed through the night as the moon shifted up in the sky, further illuminating the tree. The man watched in horror, unable to breathe, as he saw the horde of crows that covered the branches. One by one, they joined in with the others, scraping their talons against the bark. The moonlight cast their shadows on the graveyard, covering every inch of it with their twisted reflections.

The man sat frozen with fear. He tried desperately to run, but he couldn't do anything as the crows lifted their broken, distorted wings to take flight. The sound of the flapping was overwhelming, causing his ears to bleed as the crows tore through the sky, heading right for him. In an instant, they were on him, clawing into his skin, dozens at a time.

He tried desperately to scream, but he couldn't make a sound. He could do nothing but sit hopelessly as the talons tore through his flesh like razor blades. Finally the pain was too much, and he cried out into the night, but it made no difference. No one was coming to help him. He was alone.

Chapter One

Scott woke up screaming. Sweat poured down his face as he tried to catch his breath. His heart pounded inside the walls of his chest like a jackhammer as he rose up in the bed. He closed his eyes slowly, trying to calm himself down, when suddenly the sound of his alarm clock broke the silence.

He reached over to turn it off, still breathing heavily, and noticed the other side of the bed was empty. Karen must have already gone downstairs. He then moved to the edge of the bed, his feet resting on the white shag carpet beneath him, and stayed there a moment longer, still thinking about the dream. Finally, he put it behind him and stood up.

Scott walked into the bathroom, turning the light on. On the far side was a white porcelain bathtub, and past that stood a full-size mirror with a gold frame. He stood over the sink and turned the faucet on. Cold water poured out of it. He splashed it on his face, looking at his reflection. His skin was pale, contrasted by his dark black hair, now dripping with water. His eyes were a very dark brown, and as he reached down to turn the faucet off, he gave his reflection one last glance before turning to leave.

Scott knocked on April's door. "Time to get up."

April was already awake and walked to the door. Scott could hear her from the outside, taking off the locks.

The door opened and she stepped out. "Good morning, Dad," she said, smiling.

Scott was still amazed at how much she resembled her mother. Her jet-black hair was even darker than his, and it cascaded down past her shoulders. Her eyes were brown, but a bright glowing brown. Her skin was fair, with a few freckles scattered across her face, but it was offset by the darker scars on her arms. "Time for school. Go wake up the rest for me."

"Sure thing," she popped back, excited.

Scott sensed the excitement in her voice. "Don't hit Tommy with a pillow this time."

"Aww," she said, disappointed, as Scott walked down the hall towards the stairs. He couldn't help but look back at her room. His heart sank every time he saw the locks on her door. Three of them, one deadbolt and two latches. Behind them on the other side of the room sat her window, with bars resting in front of it. The kind of bars you would see in a jail cell.

Downstairs, Karen sat at the kitchen table, drinking coffee. Scott walked in and grabbed a cup. On the counter next to the coffee machine sat a dented wooden knife block with one empty slot. He filled up his cup and turned to face Karen. Her hair was messy and pulled back loosely, and her eyes had lost some of the glow that April's still had. She sat staring silently into her coffee cup, not acknowledging him. She held one hand out, rocking the crib beside her. Scott looked into the

crib and smiled at Joey, who giggled back, then he sat down opposite Karen. They sat without speaking for several minutes, until she broke the silence.

"Heard you screaming. Another bad dream?" Her voice was cold and distant.

"Yep," he replied solemnly.

"Same one as always?" she asked, still feigning interest.

Scott nodded. The room once again turned quiet as both sat looking down at the table. He wanted desperately to say something, but he couldn't find the words.

The silence was interrupted by the sound of the kids coming down the stairs. Tommy came down first. His hair was short and brown, and his skin was much less pale than Scott's. He was also a couple years younger than April, who followed him down.

She was a senior now, hoping to graduate as a valedictorian next year. She poked Tommy in the back as she walked down.

Last in line was May, the youngest except for Joey. She was only nine years old, and the black sheep of the family. Her hair was a bright blond, and her eyes were fluorescent green.

"Good morning," Karen said, now smiling as they entered the room. "Breakfast is over there."

The kids grabbed their breakfast and sat down at the table. "Anything interesting happening at school today?" Karen asked.

Tommy spoke up first. "I have a math test today," he said as he scarfed down his waffles.

"You think you're going to pass it?" she asked, curious.

"I don't think so. I couldn't even get through all the homework for it." Tommy shifted nervously in his chair.

"Don't worry about it," Scott said, trying to make him feel better. "Besides, I was never any good at math either. I don't know where your sister gets it from." Karen glared over at him but didn't say anything.

April piped in. "I can help him with the homework tonight if he needs it."

"Thanks," Tommy said.

"Anything else happening at school today?" Karen asked as she looked down into Joey's crib, cracking a smile at him.

May chimed in, "Today we are going to make drawings in art class."

"Oh, that sounds exciting," Scott said, sensing her enthusiasm. "What are you going to be drawing?"

"I'm going to draw a dog."

"What kind of dog?" April asked, looking over at her sister.

"A German shepherd, like—" Her voice choked on the last word. "Like Dakota." She looked down, trying not to cry.

April reached her hand over to May's back. Dakota had been the family dog. They had gotten him for May on her first birthday, but four months ago he'd gotten lost. "It's okay. I miss him too."

"Don't worry, we'll find him," Tommy added, trying to console her.

May looked back up at both of them and nodded.

Scott was focused on May when he noticed the clock behind her. It was 6:17. A chill went down his spine every time he saw those numbers. "Okay," he said. "The bus is almost here."

"Oh," April said. "I almost forgot. There's a parent-teacher conference in a few days."

"Okay," Scott said.

The kids got up and grabbed their backpacks. As April picked hers up, Scott noticed her putting a book inside it. "Well, I never thought I'd see the day," he joked with her.

"Ha ha," she replied sarcastically. "It's a book we have to write a paper on. I think it's Mark Twain or something."

"You know, if you give the book a chance, you may find reading isn't as torturous as you think," he replied, half-serious.

"Oh, I'm not going to read it," she said. "I just checked it out because they made us."

"If you're not going to read it, then how do you plan to write a paper on it?"

"Same way I always do." She zipped up her backpack and headed towards the door. "I'll watch the movie."

Scott walked over to the living room window, looking. The bus was turning down their street, moving toward their house. The kids waited by the door. April always smiled, but he knew she was just faking it. Inside she was nervous. He smiled back at her. Karen always stayed in the kitchen, too nervous to watch. Scott nodded at them to go as he kept watch out the window. They ran straight across the porch to the bus, but to this day he still couldn't breathe as he watched them run up to the sidewalk. For a brief moment, he saw the shotgun hidden behind the door—the one they had bought the day after it had happened. It had a wooden frame and a long gray barrel. It also had a small bloody stain on the stock, which had gone untouched for over seven years. Finally the kids made it, and they waved at him through the window. He took a deep breath as he calmed down.

"Did they make it?" Karen asked nervously from the kitchen.

"Yes," he replied as he walked back to the kitchen to grab his keys. "Oh—I have that appointment with Dr. Freeman this morning, so I'll have to stay late at work."

"Okay."

Scott leaned down into Joey's crib to say goodbye. Joey reached his hand up and grabbed his finger. He smiled down at Joey, making him giggle again, then rose, looking at his wife. "Goodbye," he said as he leaned down to kiss her cheek, but she turned away from him.

He turned to walk out of the kitchen when she decided to say something. "Have a good day at work," she said sincerely. He turned around and she smiled at him. He smiled back before walking towards the door. He stopped to look at a picture of Karen holding Joey the day he was born. He sighed to himself and walked out of the house.

Once he had left, Karen finished her coffee. Then she picked up Joey and carried him over to the living room. The ceiling fan above rocked slightly, blowing her hair as she passed under it. As she walked, a picture on the wall caught her eye. It was an old picture—one she hadn't noticed in a long time. Her eyes watered as she looked at it, remembering the day it was taken. She was wearing a navy-blue dress with two-inch white heels. Her hair was parted on the right side, cascading down the side of her face like a waterfall. She sniffled as she looked at it, then cried to herself.

Scott was driving to the therapist's office. His car was black, and the sun reflected off its metal. He passed by a field on

the side of the road. The crops had died out months ago, but he still liked the way it looked, stretching over the hills like a blanket of brown wheat. There wasn't a cloud in the sky as he turned on the radio. The weatherman came on.

"It looks like the unusually warm weather is going to continue all the way through November, with temperatures reaching the high eighties. I don't expect rainfall for at least another few weeks. The wind—" Scott turned the radio back off. He liked this warmer weather, especially this late in the year.

To the left of the road, a cedar tree stood in the distance. It had been there as long as he could remember, and it was a giant. Its branches seemed to stretch up into the sky, and its trunk was triple the width of any tree near it. Other trees were scattered up and down the road, but they were all dwarfed by it.

The tree came and went as Scott continued driving.

As he walked into the therapist's office, Dr. Freeman greeted him. "Good morning, Scott. Take a seat, I'll be just a moment."

He sat down on the couch, looking around the room. There was a large bookshelf in the corner, filled with books on every area of psychiatry. Dr. Freeman's desk sat on the adjoining side, with notes sprawled out over it. The floor was a hard granite tile, and the couch was made of black leather. The right armrest of the couch had a worn-down spot, torn almost all the way through. In the corner stood a large metal coatrack, and on the table sat a plate of donuts.

Dr. Freeman walked to the coffee machine, pouring himself a cup. He turned around, offering one to Scott, who politely declined. Scott had known Dr. Freeman for years, but now his

once greasy black hair had turned to gray, and glasses covered his eyes. He always wore a long brown overcoat, with a brown hat to match. He walked with a cane as he made his way to his chair.

"So, Scott, how have you been lately?" Dr. Freeman spoke with a deep but grandiose voice. His parents had moved from England when he was young, and he still carried a soft British accent.

"Good as can be expected," Scott said plainly. He wasn't a fan of small talk, but there wasn't much left to discuss at this point that they hadn't already gone over dozens of times. Their friendship was the main reason he still came to therapy.

"What about April? How's she doing?"

"She's managing. She acts like she's moved on, but deep down I think it still bothers her. She still keeps the locks on her door."

"Well, that's to be expected." Dr. Freeman sighed, seemingly not wanting to ask his next question. "Does she still have nightmares?"

"Sometimes. But I know what you're thinking and the answer is no. They aren't near as frequent as mine were."

Dr. Freeman looked over at him, relieved. But he had always been able to tell when someone wasn't telling him everything. "Were?"

Scott smiled, realizing he'd been caught in a lie. "Still are."

Dr. Freeman let out a soft chuckle. "You know, Scott, the nightmares are perfectly normal considering what you went through. And then with what happened to April, and then

with—what we did to—" The words caught in his throat. "What happened after April." The tension in the room had increased, and the tone of his voice grew stronger. "It's perfectly normal for the nightmares to have come back. Just so long as you remember why they started in the first place."

"Trust me," Scott said, shifting nervously in his chair. "I won't forget."

Dr. Freeman continued, not done making his point. "And so long as they don't interfere with April letting go of the past. If she sees that you can't let go of what happened to you, it will be harder for her to let go of her own past."

"I know. I try my best to hide the nightmares from the kids."

"Hiding it isn't what I meant. How can you expect her to move on when you yourself still haven't? You must at least try to let it go. If not for your sake, then for hers."

Scott nodded slowly. He knew Dr. Freeman was right, but he didn't know what to say.

They talked for a bit longer, but eventually they decided to call it a day. Scott stood up and shook Dr. Freeman's hand. "I hope you know how much I appreciate all you've done for me."

"It's always a pleasure. Plus, it is my job."

Scott chuckled. "I'll see you next month."

"Give Karen my best."

As he walked to the door, he turned back around, his tone becoming serious. "Do you ever think about it?"

Dr. Freeman looked back at him and sighed. "Every day."

Scott nodded back at him solemnly, then walked out the door.

Once Scott had left, Dr. Freeman walked over to his desk and sat down. He pulled out a picture from the bottom drawer, encased in a silver frame. He looked down at it and sighed, propping it up on his desk. He cracked a subtle smile as he sat quietly looking at the picture, which had been drawn in crayon over twenty years ago.

After a short drive, Scott arrived at work. As he walked in, he looked for Ms. Betty at the reception desk, but someone else was in her place. Ms. Betty was an older woman who had worked there longer than he had. He always spoke to her as he walked in.

"Where's Ms. Betty?" he asked the woman sitting in her place at the desk.

"She's on vacation for the week."

Scott nodded at her, then walked to the elevator. He rode it up to his floor and then headed to his office.

He stayed in his office all day, trying desperately to get enough done to head home before dark, but it was no use. He had barely made it through half of his work for the day when he noticed the clock. It was 3:45, about time for April to be calling him.

He leaned back in his chair, taking a short break as he waited for the call. The clock hit 3:55, and he started to get nervous, but after a few more minutes, his phone finally rang.

"Hello," April said on the other end of the line.

"Hey, I was waiting for you to call."

"Yeah, sorry—the bus was running a little late today, so I'm just now on our street."

"No problem at all."

They continued to talk as April, Tommy, and May walked off the bus, across the sidewalk, and into their house.

"Okay, we made it," April told Scott over the phone.

Scott breathed a sigh of relief. "Okay, honey, enjoy the rest of your day."

"I will, Dad. Love you."

"Love you too."

With that, they hung up, and Scott went back to work.

Several hours later, he finally finished everything he needed to and looked over at his clock: 11:15. He had no idea it had gotten so late. He grabbed his briefcase and headed down the elevator.

As he walked out of the building, he saw the night sky. The moon had disappeared behind clouds, making the sky pitch black. He walked across the parking lot to his car. It was the only one left in the lot. He got in, putting his seat belt on. He then turned on his headlights and headed home.

The headlights of his car cut through the darkness, lighting up the country road. The green clock in his car glowed in the darkness: 11:45 p.m. As he drove home, he looked across the side of the road at the countless trees being lit up by his headlights, appearing for only a second as he sped past them. He hated driving this road at night. It was crooked and winding, and without the view of the fields that he could see in the daytime, the drive just seemed long.

Scott was about halfway home when his head began to hurt. He tried to brush it off, but the pain only intensified.

It felt like needles digging into his scalp. Before long it was too much to bear, and he winced in pain. Suddenly, everything went black.

A few moments later, he opened his eyes, the pain having left. His vision was foggy, but he was able to make out the inside of his car. The clock glowed green, shining in his eyes: 2:47 a.m. "What?" he said, confused. When his ears stopped ringing, he heard the engine running and realized the car was still driving.

Scott almost bounced out of his seat as the car drove off the road. He looked up out of the window, seeing only black. He struggled to remain in his seat as he realized the headlights were turned off. He managed to turn them back on and they once again cut through the darkness. Only this time, they didn't light up the road but instead the cedar tree directly in front of him. He slammed on the brakes, but they did nothing. He tried to turn the wheel, but it was too late.

The car crashed into the tree, the frame buckling from the force of the impact. Scott was thrown through the windshield, colliding with the tree. He wanted to scream in pain, but he lacked the strength. He lay on the hood of his car, broken glass covering him. He was unable to move as he slowly slipped off into unconsciousness.

Chapter Two

Scott could hear people talking, but he couldn't make out the words. All he heard was a collection of voices mixed with a ringing in his ears, like a siren going off inside his head. He tried to open his eyes, but a bright light shined down in his face, blinding him.

"He's awake," a voice said.

The light above him turned off as he tried to open his eyes once more. Once his vision adjusted, he looked around the room. There were people in white clothes walking around, carrying clipboards and needles. There was a heart rate monitor on his right side, with a stethoscope hanging from it. He looked down at his forearm, seeing that a needle was stuck in it, with a tube running out of it into an IV drip.

He felt something on his face and reached up, realizing a tube was going up his nose. He grabbed it, about to pull it out, when a hand grabbed his.

"I wouldn't do that, Scott." Dr. Reynolds said, smiling at him. "I don't know why people always try to pull this out. It's not like we just stick it up your nose for no reason."

Scott laughed, but it caused his side to light up in pain. He clenched his ribs as the doctor helped him lean back. Dr. Reynolds was a tall black man and the head doctor at the hospital. His white lab coat hung all the way down to his feet.

"What happened?" Scott asked, trying to remember.

Dr. Reynolds looked at him sympathetically. "You were in a car accident."

The memories started crawling back into his mind. He could still hear the sound of the metal crashing into the tree and feel the pain of going through the windshield. "When?"

"Yesterday. It was several hours before you were found. You've lost quite a bit of blood."

"Any head trauma?"

Dr. Reynolds looked at him, surprised by the question. "Scott, you collided with a tree going eighty-five miles an hour."

"Any head trauma?" he persisted, more boldly than before.

Dr. Reynolds looked at him and smirked. "You have a cracked rib, a twisted ankle, and a few minor scratches, but, no—no head trauma."

"Are you sure?"

The doctor sighed. "Scott, the fact that you are even alive right now is a miracle. Not to mention the fact that the total extent of your injuries amounts to what I'd see from a common fender bender. And considering that you crashed out the windshield of your car and slammed into the tree directly, I would recommend that you not worry yourself about the extent of your injuries and instead thank whatever guardian angel kept you alive."

Scott nodded. The doctor was right. As he leaned up in the bed, he saw the door open. A nurse entered, leading Karen

in to see him. Her eyes were red as she ran past the doctor to embrace Scott.

"They said it looked bad," she said as she hugged him tightly, unable to hold back her tears. "I didn't think I'd see you again."

"It's okay, honey," he said as he held her. "I'm okay."

She continued to hold on to him until finally Dr. Reynolds said, "You can go home this afternoon, so long as your condition doesn't worsen in the next few hours."

"Thanks, Doc," Scott said, still looking at Karen. Despite the tears, her eyes seemed brighter than normal, as she looked back at him.

"And I hate to break up this lovely reunion, but I do have other patients that I need to attend to," Dr. Reynolds said, half-joking, as he handed them a clipboard. "Here, you'll need to fill this out."

Scott looked at the paperwork. It was the standard forms to fill out, including address, emergency contact, credit card, etc. "I thought these were usually filled out before the medical care is given," he joked back as he began filling it out.

"Per the new hospital policy, it has to be filled out by the one receiving the care, not by family members. And you couldn't very well fill it out while you were unconscious, now could you?"

Scott looked up at him, choosing to concede. "Fair point."

He handed the forms back to Dr. Reynolds, who looked them over before handing them back. "You forgot the date."

"Really?" Scott said sarcastically.

"I don't make the rules."

Scott filled out the date and handed the clipboard back. The doctor looked down at the date. November 12th. "Was that so hard?" He walked over to the door.

"Hey, Doc," Scott said, waiting for him to turn back around. "When we were here eight months ago, I thought you said you were gonna retire?"

He hesitated for a moment before answering. "I was going to but decided to push it back another year. Besides, if I retired, who'd be here to save your butt the next time you almost kill yourself?"

"Oh, so that's how it is."

"That's how it is," Dr. Reynolds chimed as he and the nurse walked out of the door. "Maybe next time wear a seat belt."

"I thought I was?" Scott asked, confused.

"Nope."

Once he had left, Scott looked over at Karen, who was now sitting in the chair beside his bed. "Where are the kids?"

"They're home. I figured April's old enough to watch them now, and I didn't want them to be up here in case—" Her voice choked on the last word as her eyes started to water again. "In case—"

"It's okay," he said as he leaned over and put his hand on her shoulder. "I'm not going anywhere."

The drive home was long. It was Karen's car, so she drove while Scott rode in the passenger seat. She listened to the radio silently, while he became lost in thought. With every tree they passed, another memory struck his head. The horrible sight of the cedar tree in front of him. The awful pain of crashing into

it. The feeling of helplessness as he lay on the hood, unable to cry out for help. But there was something else. Something he had forgotten.

He'd tried to put it out of his mind when he noticed the field on the side of the road. The sun was beginning to sink in the sky, casting an orange hue over the field. He was looking at the stalks of grain, now brown and dead, when he noticed something that hadn't been there before.

A scarecrow had been set up in the middle of the field. It was a good distance away, but he could still make out the look of it. It was hanging from a large metal stake from the ground, with its arms stretched out in a T position. It had an old cloth masking its face, and a torn brown hat sat atop its head. Underneath its brown coat were old black rags, stitched together to make a covering. Its head hung down from the stake, almost looking at the ground. Straw poured out of its hands and chest, and the stake could be seen sticking up out of its back.

Scott looked up in the sky and all around the field, searching for something, but it wasn't there. He let out a sigh of relief as he turned back to the road.

Karen heard him sigh. "What is it?"

"Oh, it's nothing," he said, trying to brush it off. "I just saw that scarecrow out over there and was wondering why they would put one out this time of year. Especially since the crops died a few months ago."

She just smiled at him and kept driving. He could tell she knew what he had been looking for, but she didn't want to push him on it. He appreciated that.

Once they reached their house, April met them at the door. "Dad!" She ran up and hugged him. Before she had let go, Tommy and May walked out too. All three embraced him. They stood hugging at the door for a moment, not saying a word, as Karen looked at them, smiling. Finally, they stopped and headed into the house.

The house looked different to Scott. April, noticing him looking, said, "Yeah, I moved some stuff around, trying to keep my mind off—well, ya know."

"I think it looks great," Karen said as she walked in.

Scott looked over at April. "Me too."

"Thanks."

They all sat down in the living room as the kids started asking questions about the accident. Karen answered their questions for Scott, sensing that he didn't want to talk about it. He looked over at April, sitting on the couch by her siblings. He noticed she had her hair pulled back in a ponytail.

She noticed him staring at her. "What?"

"It's nothing, it's just—" His voice cracked as the memory of lying on the hood of the car alone came flooding back to him. He couldn't find the words. He stood up, needing a minute to himself. "I'm going to go get a glass of water."

He was walking into the kitchen when suddenly he heard something coming from the backyard. It sounded like barking. He looked through the kitchen window to see Dakota standing in the grass, barking at the moon. Dakota's fur was brighter than a normal German shepherd's, and his eyes were a dark green. His ears perked up as he heard Scott from the house.

Scott opened the back door, calling him in. Dakota ran up to him as fast as a dog of his age could run, and Scott petted him all over. "Where've you been, boy?"

He walked back into the living room, Dakota following behind him, and looked up around the room. "When were you gonna tell me you found him?"

They all looked at each other for a moment, almost hesitating, before Karen broke the silence. "We wanted it to be a surprise."

"Yeah," Tommy added, "he showed back up yesterday before we got home from school. He was just sitting on the front porch waiting for us."

Scott leaned down to be eye level with Dakota. "Aww, you walked all the way back home." He continued to pet him, as May walked over too. "That's a good boy." Dakota sat there, enjoying the newfound attention.

After almost an hour of answering the kids' questions about the crash, along with trading off who got to pet Dakota, Scott looked around the room, realizing Joey wasn't there. He had been so distracted by the crash, and by seeing Dakota, he hadn't even noticed his playpen wasn't in the living room.

"Where's Joey?" he asked, still looking around the room.

"Joey?" Karen said in a tone that sounded almost like it was a question.

Scott looked at her, confused. "Yeah, Joey. Where is he?" He looked over to April, since she had been the one watching them. She also looked confused by the question.

He started to get nervous, until Tommy finally said, "He's upstairs."

Scott stood up, walking up the stairs and down the hallway to Joey's room. He opened it up and saw Joey wasn't there. His heart rate increased as he walked back down the hall, over to where Karen and the kids were now standing. He looked down at April, his tone growing forceful. "Where did you move Joey's crib to?"

"Crib?" she muttered to herself. "Oh," she said as her train of thought came back to her. "I moved it into the next room down."

Scott walked over, opening the door. Inside, Joey lay asleep in his crib, wrapped up in his blanket. He leaned down in the crib to look closer at him. After a moment, he walked back out of the room, shutting the door quietly so he didn't wake Joey up.

"Why didn't you just tell me you moved his crib in there?" he scolded the kids. "You had me worried."

Karen looked down at the kids, seeing they were upset. "Go easy on them. Besides, it's been a long day for all of us."

Scott nodded, realizing he was being unfair. "You're right. I guess it has been a long day." He looked down at the kids. "I'm sorry."

"It's okay, Dad."

Later that night, after everyone else had gone to sleep, Scott lay awake in bed, staring at the ceiling. He looked over at the clock. It was past midnight. He tossed and turned, trying to go to sleep, but he couldn't. Even as his eyes grew heavy, he lay there wide awake.

He looked over at Karen, sleeping beside him with her back turned. He listened to the soft sound of her breathing and looked at her long black hair, resting on the pillow beneath it.

While he was watching her sleep, hoping to drift off himself, he heard a noise coming from the window. It was so faint, he couldn't make out what it was. He was about to chalk it up to the wind when he heard it again. He got out of bed quietly, trying not to wake up Karen, and started walking over to the window as the noise grew stronger. He walked slowly, and with every step he took, the noise got louder, until he was able to make out the sound. It was the same sound he had heard so many years ago. The same sound that haunted his dreams. The sound of talons scraping against metal.

Sccrrreeee

He arrived at the window and reached up to grab the curtains as the wretched sound of scraping only grew louder. He opened the curtains and saw what was outside. On his roof stood a single crow.

Its head was slightly tilted as it stared at him through the window. Scott looked in horror at its soulless black eyes, eyes so dark it was almost as if it didn't have any. The coarse black feathers ruffled in the wind as the crow lifted up its talons and scraped them against the shingles. The horrible sound echoed throughout Scott's body as he stood there, unable to breathe.

Suddenly, the crow lifted up its wings, letting out a wicked cry so loud his ears began ringing. In an instant, it flew straight for the window, crashing into it.

Scott jumped back from the window in terror when he felt something touch his shoulder from behind. He turned around screaming but saw Karen standing there.

"What is it?" she asked as she saw he was out of breath. "What's wrong?"

He reached to point at the window, but the crow was gone. He walked over to it, looking all over the roof. There was no sign of it.

Karen looked at him, sympathetic. "Are you okay?"

Scott checked the window once more before looking back at her. He took a deep breath, trying to calm himself. "Yeah, it's just..." He paused. "I had a nightmare."

She walked over to him, holding his hand, smiling. "That's okay." She brushed her hand through his hair. "Come back to bed. You should try to get some sleep."

He nodded as she walked back over to the bed. As he turned to follow her, he looked back at the window once more. He noticed something. A hairline crack had appeared in the middle.

Scott tried to put it out of his mind as he went back to bed.

Chapter Three

Scott was eight years old when his parents had taken him to the park. They'd stayed there all day, paddling in canoes in the lake and hiking the trails. They'd had even had a picnic in the middle of the park, surrounded by the trees. It was the best day Scott had ever had, and he hadn't wanted it to end, but when it got dark, his parents said it was time to go home.

He was exhausted as they walked back through the park, heading for their car. He was a few feet behind his parents when he spotted a water fountain in the distance. He was very thirsty from hiking, so he ran over to it to get a drink.

By the time his parents finally realized he had wandered off, it was too late. They searched the entire park for him, but he was nowhere to be found.

Scott hadn't even seen the man walking up behind him.

Day 1

Scott opened his eyes to see a dark room. As his eyes focused, he saw a ray of light shining through a single window,

illuminating just enough to make out the room. It was small, barely ten feet in either direction, and Scott could see tools hanging up on the wall—hammers, screwdrivers, saws and countless others.

He looked up toward the ceiling. It was made of metal, and Scott could almost see steam coming off of it. The immense heat started to get to him as he began to breathe heavily.

Scott tried to take deep breaths, but the air was too dry. Every time he breathed in, he coughed, and every cough felt like a razor blade had been shoved down his throat.

He tried to stand up, but his head hit something. He fell back down, and as he looked around, he realized something. He wasn't just locked in the room; he was locked in a cage. A birdcage.

It was barely three feet across in each direction, the bars black but rusted. Hunched down in it, Scott leaned over to look at the door of the cage and tried to push it open, but it was locked from the outside. He reached his arms through the bars, but the rusted metal cut his hands. He jumped back in pain, hitting the back of the cage. The metal was hot, and it singed his back. He moved forward, hunched over in the middle of the cage, trying not to touch the sides.

He looked down at his hands, rust still buried in the cuts. He tried to pull it out, but it only caused him to cry out in anguish. His cries echoed off the walls of the room, so loud that it caused his ears to ring.

He tried his best to stay quiet as he sat in the cage, staying motionless for hours, until finally he heard something. He looked across the room and saw light pouring in as the

door opened. He could see the shape of a man through the light.

"Help me," Scott begged as the man walked over to him. He raised himself up as much as he could in the cage, trying to get the man's attention. "Please, help. I don't know where my mom and dad are. Where am—"

His sentence got cut short when a whip cracked against his skin through the bars of the cage. The man walked over and leaned down to be at eye level with him.

The man was wearing a loose white tank top and ripped jeans. He was very thin, and as he leaned closer, Scott could see the evil in his eyes. The man's dirty brown hair was short but ragged, and he made a strange noise with his mouth.

The man leaned closer to Scott, who started to cry. "Well, well, well, it appears my little bird wants to fly away from home." The man spoke with a coarse Southern accent. "Now just what do you think we need to do about that?" He cracked a sinister smile.

Scott stayed back in the corner of the cage, watching as the man stood back up. The man walked over to the corner of the room, grabbed a metal dog dish and poured a handful of water in it, setting it in the cage. "Drink up."

The man turned around and walked out of the room, shutting the door. Darkness once again flooded the room. Scott looked down at the water bowl. He reached his hands down and raised water up to his mouth. It was warm, and filled with what tasted like dirt, but he was so thirsty he drank it anyway.

The hours felt like days as Scott waited in the cage, trying not to give up hope. He kept telling himself that it wasn't real,

that he was just having a nightmare. He told himself that soon he would wake up, and his mom and dad would be there to comfort him. But deep down he knew it wasn't true.

Soon, night came, and the light disappeared from the window. Despite the water, he was still dehydrated from the heat. He lay down sideways, curled into a ball because there wasn't enough room to spread out. *I just have to go to sleep*, he told himself as he drifted off. *Then when I wake up, everything will be okay.*

Sccrrreeee

The horrific sound woke Scott up. It was still the middle of the night, and the darkness consumed his vision. He heard it again. He was wide awake now, shaking in fear. The haunting sound continued to pour into the room as he listened, trying to figure out what it was. It sounded like something scraping across the roof, almost as if something was walking across it.

Sccrrreeee

The sound intensified, and Scott thought he could hear more footsteps crawling their way across the roof. The scraping echoed against the wall, infinitely louder than before. The sound was so great that he could feel his ears bleed.

Sccrrreeee

Every time Scott thought the sound had disappeared, it would come back worse, growing louder, more frenzied. His imagination ran wild. What monstrous creature could be walking right above him? What if it had long claws, or sharp teeth? What if it had coarse black fur instead of skin, or horns jutting out from where its ears should have been?

The sound had grown even louder, as if dozens of claws were ripping into the roof at the same time. Scott couldn't breathe as he sat in the cage, waiting for the creature to come down through the window and find him. He kept his eye trained on the window, despite it being too dark to see.

Scott sat awake the entire night, listening to the horrific sound, waiting to die.

Day 2

Daylight had come, and the sound had stopped. The door opened and the man walked in again. He had his black whip in one hand and a bottle of water in the other. He walked over to the cage and leaned down.

The man made a strange noise with his lips as he looked at Scott, who backed into the corner, cowering. "You look tired, my boy," he said as he poured the water into the dog pail. "Trouble sleeping, I take it?"

Scott said nothing, instead waiting for the man to leave so he could drink the water. The man pushed the dog pail closer to him. "By all means, boy, don't wait on my account."

The man stood up to leave. Scott had picked up the bowl to pour it in his mouth when he heard the crack of a whip. It tore through the bars of the cage, slicing his arm. He dropped the bowl and the water spilled out everywhere.

The man was smirking. "Aww, would you look at that? You dropped your bowl." He gave a faint chuckle and left.

Scott sat clutching his arm as the blood dripped down from it, mixing with the water on the floor.

Day 4

Night had come once again. Scott lay sideways in the cage, trying to sleep, but the sound came back. The horrific scraping haunted him every night as it echoed off the walls, finding him in the darkness. He stayed focused on the window until the moon finally became just bright enough for him to see something. It sat in the windowsill, but he couldn't make out what it was. All he could see was the moonlight reflecting off its eyes—dark, twisted eyes.

Sccrrreeee

Day 7

Scott was starving to death. He could feel his ribs protruding through his skin as he lay in the cage. The sun was shining through the window, but he lacked the strength to sit up. His mouth was dry. He reached over for the water pail, pulled it to his side, and tipped it up into his mouth, but it was empty. Not a drop of water was left. He let it fall back down as he gave up hope. He lay there silently, waiting to die. Almost wanting to.

The door slammed open. The man walked in, carrying a bag. Scott opened his eyes, his vision blurry. The man walked over and set the bag down by the cage.

"Well, well," the man said as he made the same strange sound, almost like he was sucking his teeth. "It does appear as if my little bird has seen better days." The man held his hand to his chest. "I blame myself. I have been a bad owner. I have not properly nourished you. But don't you worry about that." The man knelt down beside the cage, putting another pail inside. With a condescending tone, he added, "I do solemnly swear to remedy this error immediately."

Scott's vision returned to him and he saw the bag more clearly. It was large, with writing all over it. The outside of the bag was bright blue, with a picture in the middle. A blue jay.

It was birdseed.

The man opened the bag up and poured it into the pail, letting it spill over onto the floor. It smelled horrible, but Scott didn't care. He reached over, grabbing a handful. His mouth was so dry, the seed cut into it as he ate it, causing him to wince in pain.

"Aww, is it a little rough?" The man opened a water bottle and poured water on it before pouring the rest in the water pail. "There, that should soften it up." Scott continued to eat it as the guy watched him, waiting for a response. "What do you say, boy?" Scott looked up at him, confused. The man held the whip up, raking it against the bars. "What do you say?"

Scott looked at him in fear. "Thank you."

"You are most certainly welcome." With that, the man left, leaving Scott all alone, eating the birdseed out of the pail.

Day 19

Scott hadn't slept in four days. The moon was full in the sky, illuminating the window. The creatures had returned to the roof, walking back and forth across it. Scott listened as the creatures dragged their claws on the metal above him. Suddenly, something darted past the window. Scott looked over, but it was gone in an instant. He waited for it to come back. Finally he saw it again, but there were more this time. Streaks of black tore past the window like ghosts, flying in random directions. Scott watched in horror as one flew straight into the window, breaking it.

The creature was inside now with Scott, who screamed at the top of his lungs. The monstrous creature beat its wings, flying back and forth across the ceiling, too fast for him to make out what it was. Finally, it flew back out the window, leaving Scott in the cage, alone, crying to himself.

Day 27

The man walked into the room, slamming the door behind him. Scott jumped back against the walls of the cage, not knowing what was happening. The man stormed in in a rage and walked over to the cage, pulling him out of it. He threw him down to the floor and started whipping him. Scott begged him to stop, but the man didn't. With every crack of the whip, his back lit up in pain. He let out an

awful cry, as he could feel his flesh being ripped from his body.

"Why are you doing this?" he cried out as his back became soaked with blood. He could feel it streaming down his back. It felt warm.

The man said nothing, instead continuing to beat him until finally he threw him back into the cage and locked the door once again. Scott lay down in the cage, bleeding.

Day 42

The cuts had finally scarred over, but Scott's back still ached whenever it hit the bars of the cage. He lay down to try to sleep. The creatures still kept him up at night, so now he tried to sleep during the day. But even then, the horrific scraping haunted his dreams. But this time, it wasn't the nightmares that woke him up. It was the sound of the whip cracking.

The man pulled him out of the cage once more and began to torture him again. The whip cracked against the scars, opening up his back. Scott cried out in pain every time the whip cracked, but his screams of agony availed nothing. He was forced to lie there helplessly as he was tormented.

The man finished and knelt down to look him in the eye as he lay on the floor, drenched in blood. "Sorry, boy, but sometimes you have to remind your bird who their master is. You understand, boy?"

Scott said nothing as he lay there, barely alive.

The man repeated himself, louder this time. "Do you understand?"

Scott nodded his head slightly, and the man stood back up. "Good."

The man picked him up and threw him back into the cage. He slammed the door to the cage shut and walked out the door. Scott lay there for almost an hour until finally he gathered his strength and sat upright in the cage. That was when he noticed something. The man had forgotten to put the lock on the cage.

Scott sat in the cage, looking at the unlocked door. He wanted so badly to open it and run out of the room, but he didn't know what was on the other side. The fear kept him in the cage for hours. *What if the creatures are still out there?* he thought. *What if the man catches me?*

He felt the blood dry on his back as he thought of his parents. How much he wanted to get out of here and see them again. He thought of how he would probably die if he was trapped here much longer. About the rancid taste of the bird food he was forced to eat, and the handful of water he was forced to make last days at a time. As those thoughts flooded his mind, he mustered his strength and reached over, pushing the cage door open.

He ran out of the cage and over to the door of the room. He hesitated for a moment before letting go of his fear and opening it. As he stepped out, he felt grass crunch beneath his feet and saw a house across the yard. Beyond that, a field stretched out for what seemed like miles.

He turned around to look where he'd been trapped. It was a shed, sitting in the corner of the backyard. He took one

last look, then started running through the field, behind the backyard.

Scott ran as fast as he could. Stalks of grain hit his knees as he kept going for what seemed like hours, until finally his breath gave out. He looked over the horizon of the field and saw a road. He caught his breath for a minute and started to run again.

His vision was so focused on the road, he almost ran into the scarecrow in front of him. The scarecrow was plain, its cloth body filled with straw. It was tied up to a post.

He stopped to look at it when he saw something dart behind it in the sky. It was the same streak of black he'd seen break through the window that night. He heard its awful screech as he saw more soar down from the sky. They flew all around him as he collapsed on the ground in fear. They darted back and forth right above his head as he crawled back, leaning on the scarecrow, hoping it would scare them off. It didn't.

They seemed to multiply by the thousands as he watched them soar above him, covering the sky like the black veil of a mourning bride. Each one of them let out their own unique cry. The combined sound was bloodcurdling as Scott sat in the field alone, screaming for help.

Then the creatures dove down, headed straight for him.

Chapter Four

Scott lay in bed awake as his alarm clock rang. He sat up and reached over to turn it off. Karen had already gone downstairs to start breakfast for the kids, but he had stayed in bed, hoping to get at least a little sleep before work. Instead he had lain wide awake, thinking about the crow.

After a few minutes, he got out of bed and reached over to the nightstand to grab his phone, but it wasn't there. He looked down, confused, then realized he hadn't seen his phone since the accident. It must've gotten lost in the crash. He looked over to Karen's side of the bed and saw his old phone sitting on her nightstand. He reached over and grabbed it before walking into the bathroom.

Inside, he dialed Dr. Freeman as he splashed cold water on his face. The phone rang but went to voicemail.

"Hey, Doc, this is Scott. I know we just had a session two days ago, but I was in a car wreck. The doctor said I was fine, but I saw something weird last night, so I was hoping we could set up a session sometime this week if you're not too busy. No rush, just call me back when you have time."

Scott hung up the phone and stared at his reflection in the mirror. He didn't know how he was going to tell Dr. Freeman about seeing the crow, but he knew he needed to.

Scott got dressed and walked down the hall to April's room. He knocked on the door and waited for the sound of locks being turned, but there was none. The door opened, and he looked in disbelief. All the locks had been removed. He cut his eyes behind April, looking back at the windows, and saw there were no bars across them either.

April looked at him, confused by his expression. "What?"

"You took the locks down?" he said, hoping it was true.

She hesitated for a moment before answering, "Yeah, I thought it was time."

Overwhelmed by joy, Scott hugged her, lifting her off the ground. His eyes watered as he thought of how far she'd come. How she had finally been able to move on, something he hadn't been able to do himself.

"Okay, Dad, what's going on?" April asked innocently.

He let go of her but kept his hand on her shoulder. "It's just—I'm proud of you."

She smiled. "Aww, thanks."

They stood there for a moment, not knowing what to say, until finally he winked at her. "Go wake up the others for me."

"Sure thing," she said as Scott walked toward the stairs.

"And, honey..."

She listened, expecting him to say something about how she was moving on, or how much he loved her.

He knew what she was thinking. "You can hit Tommy with a pillow this morning."

That was even better.

As Scott walked into the living room, he saw Dakota sitting on the rug, wagging his tail. "Hey, boy," he said as he knelt down to pet him. "It's good to have you back."

He stood back up and walked into the kitchen. He walked over to get a cup of coffee as Karen walked up behind him. He felt her hand on his back as he turned around to see her when she greeted him with a kiss.

"Good morning," she said as she looked up into his eyes.

"Good morning," he replied, slightly confused.

"How did you sleep?" She smiled at him and wrapped her arms around his back.

Scott hesitated for a moment before responding. Her voice seemed sincere. "Uh, actually I didn't?"

"Really?" she said as she let go and grabbed her own cup of coffee. "Not at all?"

He shook his head and sat down at the table as she walked over to grab Joey from his crib. Her hair was brushed neatly, falling down her back. Her eyes were radiant, and she was smiling brightly.

She noticed him staring and turned to see if he was looking at something behind her. "What?"

Scott smiled at her. "Nothing, it's just—you look beautiful today."

She smiled as she picked Joey up and carried him over to the table. She sat down in the chair, rocking him back and forth, as Scott watched. It was nice seeing her like this.

"Oh," she said, remembering, "did you see the phone I set out?"

"Yeah, thanks." Scott sipped his coffee and looked back over at her. "Did you know April took the locks down from her door?"

Karen looked back over at him, excited. "That's great."

As she said that, Scott heard the kids coming down the stairs. He looked over and saw May stop in the living room to pet Dakota.

"Good morning," he said as the kids walked in.

Karen motioned to the counter. "Breakfast is over there."

The kids walked over to get it and then sat down. Scott looked over at April, still proud of her. She cut her eyes toward him, noticing him staring again. He saw her notice and stopped.

"How did your math test go?" Scott asked Tommy.

Tommy shifted in his chair, thinking for a moment before replying. "It went good."

"Really?" Scott asked, surprised. "What did you make on it?"

"A," he answered in between bites.

"Wow, that's great." Scott noticed Tommy's voice was quieter than normal as he held up his hand, high-fiving him. "I guess April won't have to tutor you after all."

"Yeah, I guess I'm the smart one now," Tommy joked. He looked over at April.

She rolled her eyes at him. "Please, you were five before you could tie your shoes."

"That is a blatant lie," he snapped back sarcastically. "You're just mad 'cause now you have some competition."

April looked over to see Tommy smiling. She flicked her fork at him, causing syrup to fly off and hit his face.

Tommy looked back at her defiantly as he wiped the syrup off and proceeded to lick it from his fingers. "Is that the best you got?"

She picked up her fork again, before Karen stopped them. "Alright, that's enough fun for this morning."

April put the fork down slowly and they both went back to eating.

Scott noticed May taking food off her plate and sneaking it down to Dakota, just like April used to do. "Does Dakota like the eggs?"

May looked up, realizing she'd been caught. "Umm," she said, trying to think of a way out of it.

"It's okay, sweetie," Karen said as she and Scott looked over at her. "I'm sure Dakota's hungry too."

Tommy picked up a biscuit and threw it to him. Karen looked over at him, smirking. "Don't push it."

Everyone went silent for a moment before April smiled to herself. She reached over and literally pushed the plate.

Everyone laughed for a moment until they heard Joey giggle in Karen's arms.

"Aww," Scott said, looking at April, "Joey thinks you're funny."

Karen rocked Joey back and forth in her arms as he continued to giggle.

"Can I hold him?" April asked as she stood up and walked over to Karen. Karen handed Joey off to her, and April walked around the room, rocking him back and forth.

As she rocked Joey, Scott spoke to Tommy. "Seriously, though, I am proud of you on the A."

"Thanks, Dad."

Scott looked over at May, whose plate wasn't on the table anymore. She held it down under the table, letting Dakota lick it clean. Karen was looking back toward April and didn't see May. May looked at Scott, thinking she would be in trouble. He motioned his head toward Karen and held his finger up to his lips. He mouthed *shh*, and she mouthed it back.

By the time Karen turned back around, the plate was back up on the table, with only a piece of egg left on it.

They continued to talk, until they all finished their breakfast. Karen stood up to grab the plates. When she grabbed May's, she reached for the piece of egg left on it.

"Wait, no," Scott blurted, but it was too late. She ate it.

She stopped and looked back at Scott. "What?"

Scott, Tommy and May started to laugh.

"What?" she repeated.

Scott shook his head slightly. "Nothing."

She continued to look at them for a moment before moving on. Scott glanced at May and smiled at her.

Once Karen had left the room, April looked over at them, confused. "What was so funny?"

Tommy answered. "May had let Dakota lick off that plate."

"Seriously?" April said, trying not to laugh, but failing.

Scott nodded as he saw the clock behind them: 6:17. He sighed. "Time for school."

The kids stood up and grabbed their backpacks. Karen came back in as they started to walk to the door. April opened the door to walk outside when Scott stopped her, his forehead wrinkled with confusion.

"Wait till it gets here."

"Okay," April said, confused herself.

The bus finally arrived, and the kids walked out to it. Scott was watching through the window when he felt Karen's hand on his back. He glanced at her, surprised, but then looked back towards the kids. They made it on the bus okay, and then Scott turned toward Karen.

"What is it?" she asked, sensing Scott's confusion.

He smiled. "Nothing, it's just been a while since you were like this."

"Like what?"

Scott looked into her eyes. "Happy."

"Really?" she said to herself before smiling back at him like he hadn't seen her smile in years.

Scott looked back at the clock, knowing it was time for him to go to work. "I'm going to have to borrow your car, if that's okay."

She looked at him playfully. "Very well. Just be gentle with her."

"Yes, ma'am." Scott grabbed her keys to walk out the door. As he did, he looked at the pictures on the wall. He stopped for a moment, surprised.

"Where is the picture of Joey?"

"Which one?" Karen asked.

"The one of you and him at the hospital—you know, the day he was born."

Karen looked at the wall with him, searching for it. "I don't know, I guess April moved it when she was rearranging the house."

"You're probably right," he said as he leaned down to kiss her goodbye.

"Have a good day at work, honey," she said, winking at him.

He smiled back and walked to the car.

On the way to work, Scott had the radio turned on. It was set to an oldies station, so he changed it to news, but all he got was static. Typical, he thought as he switched channels and listened to the weatherman, hoping the warm weather would continue.

"We will be seeing lots of rainfall in the next few weeks, with temperatures still in the mid- to low sixties. Chance of severe thunderstorms later this week, with—"

Scott turned it off, disappointed. He continued to drive, and as he looked back across the field, he saw the scarecrow again. It seemed closer to the road this time, and its head hung lower on the spike than before. Wind blew leaves through the field, which passed by the scarecrow, almost circling around it. Some leaves caught in the rips of the brown coat. He looked for a moment but thought nothing of it as he continued to drive toward work.

He walked into his office building, and to his surprise, Ms. Betty sat at the reception desk. Her hair was gray, and brown glasses covered her eyes.

"I thought you were on vacation?" Scott asked as he walked by her.

"I was," she replied. "But a storm came and I had to cut it short."

"That's too bad."

She nodded her head in response.

As he turned to walk to the elevator, he looked back at her. "New glasses today. You look good."

"Why, thank you," she said, blushing.

Scott rode in the elevator up to his floor. The elevator's walls were colored velvet red, and the floor wooden. The faint sound of elevator music rang down from the speakers.

Soon he reached his floor and walked into his office. He sat down at his desk and started working.

After looking through files all day, he looked at the clock: 3:45. He leaned back in his chair, setting his phone on the desk, and took a short break to wait for April to call. He waited for a while before he started to get worried. It was 4:05 now and she still hadn't called.

He leaned over and picked up his cell phone to call her. He held the phone up to his ear as it started ringing. As it kept ringing on the other end of the line, he started to get nervous. Each ring felt like a lifetime to Scott as he waited for her to answer, but she didn't, until finally it went to voicemail.

"Hey, April, it's Dad." His voice was cracking. "I was just calling to see if you were okay, so just please call me back when you can."

A few seconds later, his phone rang, and he heard April's voice. "Dad?"

"Hey, honey. Are you okay?"

"Yes?" she said, sounding confused. "Why wouldn't I be?"

"You didn't call."

"Oh." Her voice returned to normal. "Yeah, sorry, I completely forgot."

Scott sighed to himself, relieved. "It's okay, just please remember next time."

"Okay, Dad, I will. Love you."

"Love you too." With that, he hung up the phone. He looked back over at the files on his desk and started to finish some of them off. He hoped to get home earlier today.

After another hour or so, he had finished enough paperwork to leave for the day, so he stood up from his desk and grabbed his briefcase. As he was about to walk out, his door opened.

Scott looked over to the door to see Kyle standing in the doorway. "Got a sec?"

Scott looked down at his watch. "Sure, man, what's up?"

Kyle walked in and closed the door. "First off, I heard about the crash. I wanted to see if you were okay."

"Yeah, I'm fine."

"Really?" Kyle asked. "No injuries or anything? It sounded pretty rough."

"Yeah, I have a couple scratches but nothing serious."

"Wow. I guess you must've had a guardian angel looking after you."

Scott chuckled to himself.

"What?"

Scott smiled. "Nothing, it's just the doctor said something similar." He looked at his watch again, wanting to get home. "Was there anything else?"

"Yeah," Kyle said, as he held up a brown envelope. "Boss wants you to look at these numbers."

"Boss?" Scott questioned. "It's not enough you get the promotion, now you're referring to yourself in third person?"

"Ha ha," Kyle laughed sarcastically. "My boss wants you to look at these. It's no rush, though."

Scott looked at the envelope before setting it on his desk. "Okay, but you know I don't crunch numbers anymore. I just do paperwork now."

"I'm sure you can make one exception," Kyle said, slapping him on the arm.

"Okay," he said as he opened the door to his office. "I'll try to look at them tomorrow."

Kyle nodded, and they both walked out the door.

Scott got home just in time for dinner. As he stepped into the house, he was pounced on by Dakota.

"I missed you too, boy," he said as he scratched Dakota's back, causing his back legs to shake back and forth. "You haven't done that in a while."

The kids came down to greet Scott as they made their way to the dinner table.

As Scott walked to the kitchen to wash his hands, Karen came up behind him, kissing him on the neck and resting her head on his shoulders. "How'd your day go?"

He squinted at her. "It went good."

"That's good." Karen walked over to the stove to get the lasagna out of the oven. Steam rose up from the dish as the smell drifted through the house. Scott could almost taste it from across the room.

The kids had all sat down at their places at the table. April and Tommy sat across from each other, with May sitting on

Tommy's side, closest to Scott. Scott sat down at the end of the table as Karen placed the lasagna in the middle of the table before sitting down opposite Scott, with Joey's bassinet beside her.

They passed the dish back and forth, each taking scoops out onto their own plate. Scott served May's for her as Dakota reached his head up to the table.

"No," Karen said before May could ask to give some to Dakota. "He can have the leftovers."

Scott set the dish back in the middle of the table, and they all began eating. He took a bite of the lasagna. "This tastes great."

The kids nodded in agreement as Karen smiled. "Thank you."

Scott continued to eat the food, amazed by how good it tasted. The cheese mixed with the sauce as the meat melted in his mouth. He finished his first serving within minutes and grabbed another.

"So how was school?" he asked the kids.

April had stopped eating and was now playing with her food. "Same as always."

Karen entered the conversation. "What about you, Tommy? You still doing good in math?"

"Yeah, I'm doing okay."

"That's good. Anything interesting happen today?"

May's mouth was full when she joined in. "Tommy pushed me on the swings at recess."

"Don't talk with your mouth full, baby," Karen added softly.

"Sorry, Mom."

"So Tommy pushed you on the swings." Scott looked over at Tommy, winking at him. "That must've been fun."

"Uh-huh," May said, nodding her head.

April looked over at her. "How high did you go?"

May held her hand up in the air as far as she could.

"Oh wow," April said, smiling at her. "That's pretty high."

She shook her head up and down, happy to be getting attention.

Scott looked over at her, remembering something. "Oh, you were supposed to draw an art project for school, right?" May nodded. "Can I see it?"

May leapt out of the chair to go grab the picture. While they waited for her to come back, they continued to eat.

"What was she supposed to draw again?" Karen asked Scott.

"I think she said her favorite animal," he said as he took another bite of food.

"There she is," April said as May walked up behind Scott, holding the picture for him to see.

Scott looked at it before choking on his food. He coughed, trying to clear his throat. A single crow, drawn in crayon. Its feathers stretched out over the page, with its eyes gray and lifeless. Its talons rested at the bottom of the page, and its head sat tilted on its body.

Scott took a second to catch his breath as his heart rate increased. "I thought you were going to draw a dog, like Dakota?"

"I changed my mind," May said as she looked at his frightened expression, her eyes starting to water. "Do you like it?"

The rest of the family looked at him as he tried to control his breathing. He looked over at May. "I do like it, honey, very much. It's just—" No matter how hard he tried, he couldn't get

the words to come out. "Excuse me," he said as he stood up and walked into the living room.

Scott paced the floor with his head in his hands. His adrenaline was racing as he thought of the picture and how detailed it was. The black feathers stuck in his mind as he remembered the awful sound. The way they flew past the window of the shed. The way they dove at him. He sat down on the couch, his hand covering his face. "What's wrong with you?" he muttered to himself.

"Dad," April said as she walked into the room. "Are you okay?" She walked over to the couch and sat down beside him. She put her hand around his shoulders as she looked into his eyes, seeing the fear in them. "Dad?"

"Yeah," he said, looking over at her. "I'm fine. Just bad memories."

"The crow?"

Scott nodded.

"You want to talk about it?"

"No, that's okay," he said as he patted her on the back softly.

She smiled at him as she leaned her head down on his shoulder. "You know, Dad, May is pretty upset in there. She thinks you didn't like the drawing."

He sighed. "I guess I did react pretty badly, didn't I?"

"Yep," April said plainly.

"Think she'll forgive me?" he joked.

"Probably, but it wouldn't hurt to try bribing her with ice cream."

"Excellent idea," Scott said as he stood up. As they walked back into the kitchen, he turned to April, his voice becoming serious. "Thank you."

Scott walked into the kitchen. "Who wants ice cream?"

The family sat in the living room, eating the ice cream. After a while, April pointed to a picture on the wall. "What were you and Mom doing there?"

Scott looked up at the picture. "That's actually from our first date."

"Ohh," April said. "Tell us."

Scott looked up at the picture as the memories came flooding back to him. "Well, I had asked your mom out to a movie."

"And then what happened?" April asked.

"We went to see a movie."

"That's it?" Karen asked as she cut her eyes over to Scott. "We went to see a movie?"

"What?" he asked, confused.

"That's all you remember?" Tommy asked.

"Yeah," he said, trying to defend his point. "We went to see a movie, I put my arm around her, it was a date."

April looked at her dad. "That's just sad."

"What about that one?" May chimed in, pointing to another picture on the wall.

Scott looked up at it, seeing which picture it was. "I'll have to let your mom take this one. I don't really remember that picture."

"Like you remembered the other one?" April said sarcastically.

"Watch yourself," Scott said, chuckling.

Karen looked at the picture on the wall. "Well, it was our fifth date, and we went to the park to have a picnic. We had grilled cheese sandwiches with sour cream potato chips, and a few extra chocolate chip cookies for dessert. We had gotten there late, so by the time we finished eating, the sun was setting.

"The light from the sun was shining off my hair as we spread out the blanket to lie on it. I was wearing a bright red sundress, with flowers on it, and mismatched gold earrings."

"Kinda fancy for the park," April said.

"I was also wearing sneakers." The kids started laughing.

"The wind was blowing, so my hair was a complete mess. Your father brushed it out of my eyes right as the sun went down completely, and the stars lit up the sky."

"How many stars were there?" Scott joked.

"Seven hundred and forty-two," Karen snapped back sarcastically, not paying him any attention. "We lay there for hours, looking up at the stars, your father pointing out the constellations." Karen smiled.

"What was Dad wearing?" April asked, curious.

"He was wearing a light blue polo shirt, with three buttons down the middle and a mustard stain on the left shoulder. He had on jeans that were slightly faded on the left side, and his hair was looser than how he has it now."

"Wow," Scott said as he looked over at Karen in amazement. "That was specific."

"What? It was a good date," she said, smiling.

"Sounds like it."

Once they had all finished their ice cream, Scott looked at the clock. It was getting late. "Time for bed." As he stood up, his arm suddenly felt warm.

"Dad?" he heard April say. He saw the haunting expression on their faces and looked down to see that blood was running down his forearm.

Scott winced in pain as Karen ran to get a hand towel. The kids stood up, trying to figure out how to help. Blood continued to stream down his arm, covering his hand and dripping from his fingers onto the floor. It felt so warm on his skin.

Karen came back with the hand towel as Scott finally stopped bleeding. She began to wipe off the blood that was on his arm, the towel becoming drenched in red.

Finally, Karen got it all wiped off. Tommy tried to use the towel to scrub the blood off the carpet, but it just spread it out more.

Scott looked at his arm, noticing a hairline cut right on his elbow joint. He looked at it, trying to figure out how he hadn't noticed it before.

"It's probably from the crash," Karen said, trying to reassure him. "Doctors just must not have noticed it."

Scott shook his head. "You're probably right. I'll call Dr. Reynolds tomorrow to ask about it," he said as he looked down at the circles of red staining the carpet.

A little while later, the kids had gone upstairs to bed. Karen picked Joey up from his bassinet and rocked him back and forth in her arms. She walked over beside Scott, hugging him

on the side with her free arm. "The crow wasn't the only thing that bothered you about that picture, was it?"

He closed his eyes for a second as the image came back to him. "No. No, it wasn't."

Scott lay in bed awake. It had been several hours, but he still couldn't sleep. His thoughts kept drifting back to the picture. The crow, with its twisted feathers and lifeless eyes. He tried not to think back to the shed, back to when they haunted him every night, but the memories wouldn't go away.

All he could think of was how innocent May had looked holding up a picture of it, unaware of what it meant to him. But there was something else bothering him too.

The insane detail of the picture. May wasn't bad at drawing by any stretch, but this was different. It was drawn in crayon, and yet it almost looked like a photograph. Every single minute detail was perfect, right down to the hollow darkness of its eyes. The thought that it had been drawn by May sent a chill down his spine.

Scott stared at the ceiling, knowing he wasn't going to be able to fall asleep. He decided to get up and splash some water on his face and try to think. He tried to rise up in the bed, but he didn't move. He tried again, this time trying to move his arms, but once again he was unable to. He was paralyzed.

He began fighting, desperately trying to move even an inch, but he couldn't. He was forced to lie there in the bed, motionless. He tried to open his mouth to scream, but no sound came out. His heart pounded in his chest, feeling like

it might burst. He tried to catch his breath, but every breath burned like fire in his lungs.

Finally, after several minutes of pain, he was able to move. He sat up in the bed, gasping for air. He was lightheaded, and sweat dripped down from his hair.

"Scott?" Karen asked, waking up.

He looked over at her, not saying a word.

She sat up in the bed beside him. "What's wrong?" she said, seeing the fear in his eyes and putting her arm around his back. "Did you have another nightmare?"

"No, it wasn't just..." He paused. "I hadn't gone to sleep."

"Then what was it?" There was sympathy in her voice. "You can tell me."

He looked over at her, seeing how concerned she was. "It's nothing. I think I'm just tired from not sleeping. Must be seeing things."

"Are you sure?"

Scott nodded and stood up, walking into the bathroom. He turned the water on, splashing it onto his face. The cold water felt refreshing as it dripped from his hair.

He looked up at his reflection in the mirror, noticing a small cut on his cheek. He raised his hand up to it, but he didn't feel it there. When he looked back at the mirror, it was gone.

Joey started crying.

Karen rose to go check on him, but Scott stopped her. "I got it." He leaned over to kiss her goodnight.

"Have fun," she said as she lay back down.

Scott walked down the hallway. He tried to put what had just happened out of his mind and calm himself down as he

approached Joey's room. He grabbed the doorknob, but it wouldn't turn. He tried again, but still nothing.

Joey's cries grew louder as Scott struggled to open the door. He banged against the door with his shoulder, but it wouldn't budge. He started to panic as Joey's cries grew worse. It didn't just sound like his normal crying anymore. It sounded like something was wrong.

The door finally gave way, revealing the room inside, dimly lit by a nightlight in the corner. Scott rushed in to get Joey. He picked Joey up as he let out a sigh of relief. After a few moments, Joey stopped crying and rested in his arms.

He rocked Joey back and forth for a while, making sure he was asleep, then walked back to the crib and reached to put Joey down in it. That was when he saw something. A single black feather underneath Joey's blanket.

Scott stepped back in horror as the sound of scratching claws entered the room. He was still holding Joey in his arms as he looked out the window. A crow sat on the other side, scraping its talons against the roof. Its head was tilted almost sideways as it looked in at Scott. Suddenly, the crow lifted up its foot and raked its talons across the window, tearing into the glass. Scott stepped back against the wall as the crow continued to scrape its claws against the glass, the horrific sound echoing throughout the room.

Sccrrreeee

With his back to the wall, Scott's legs buckled underneath him, and he dropped to the floor, landing with his back against the wall. Joey, still in his arms, began crying again as he sat frozen in fear, staring at the crow on the other side of the window, listening to the nightmarish scraping.

Chapter Five

The sun was coming up in the sky as Karen walked into Joey's room. Seeing Scott on the floor holding Joey in his arms, she rushed over to him. "What's wrong?"

His eyes were glazed over as he looked into the distance.

She put her hand on his cheek. "What happened?"

He didn't say a word, instead lifting up his hand and pointing at the window, which was covered in deep scratches.

She looked at the window and then turned back to face him. "What is it?"

Scott looked at her in disbelief. He pointed to the window again. "The scratches."

She looked back at him with sympathy. "There's nothing on the window, Scott."

He stood up, handing Joey to her. He walked over to the window and saw that the scratches were gone. "That's not possible," he muttered to himself.

"Are you okay?" she asked.

"The feather," he said, remembering. He walked over to the crib to show her the feather in it, but it was gone as well. He held his hands up to his face. "No, no, no."

"Scott?" Karen walked over to him, putting her spare arm on his. "What's wrong?"

He looked into her eyes, not knowing what to say.

"Did you see something? A crow?"

He nodded as she put Joey back in the crib.

"Scott, you haven't slept in days. You're probably just seeing things." Karen walked over and put her arm around him.

He held her back, but he continued to stare at the window in disbelief.

She let go of Scott and walked back toward the door.

"Karen?"

"Yes?"

He hesitated, not knowing how to ask this. "Do the kids seem different to you?"

Her eyes widened as she stepped closer. "Different how?"

He shook his head and sighed. "I don't know, it's just..."

"It's just what?" Karen looked at him, waiting for his response.

Scott could tell she was concerned by his question. "It's just..." He struggled to get the words out. "It's just, there's something off, but I can't place it."

She walked back over to him, reaching up to touch the side of his face. "Maybe you should take the day off work. Stay home, try and get some sleep."

Scott shook his head. "It's not that, it's just... something is off, I can feel it. Especially Tommy."

"Okay," she said, looking him in the eyes. "I think you're tired, and I think you're seeing things that aren't there. Why don't you go see Dr. Freeman? Maybe he can help you with whatever this is."

"I tried calling him already, but he didn't answer. I'll try again this morning."

"Good," Karen said as she raised herself up to kiss Scott. "Now come downstairs, I have breakfast ready."

Downstairs, Scott sat at the table, eating breakfast alongside Karen and the kids. Karen rocked Joey in her arms as he looked around at the kids, who were eating their breakfast like normal. He watched them each for a moment, feeling guilty that he had even thought that there was something off about them. They looked so happy, eating and talking with each other. *I must be going crazy*, he thought as he looked down at his food.

"You seem quiet, Dad," April said. "Is something wrong?"

"No, everything's fine. Just tired, that's all."

Suddenly, Scott thought of something. He didn't even want to consider it; the very thought sent chills down his spine. And it didn't make sense, he told himself. It was impossible. Unless...

"What day is it?"

"What?" Karen asked, surprised.

"What is the date?" Scott repeated.

"Uhh," Karen said, trying to think.

"Fourteenth," Tommy said. "I think it's the fourteenth."

"So the crash was three days ago, right. Only three days?"

"Yeah," April said, confused. "Why?"

"No reason." Scott breathed a sigh of relief. He put the thought out of his head and continued eating.

April's skin looked fairer, and she had her black hair pulled back in a ponytail again.

April noticed him looking. "What?"

"Your hair looks good like that," Scott said.

April brushed her hair with her hand. "Aww, thanks, Dad."

Karen looked over at her too. "It does look good like that. You used to always wear it that way. Why did you change?"

"I don't know," April said, grinning ear to ear. "I guess I'll keep it this way."

"Uhh, I don't know," Tommy joked. "Maybe it would look better hanging down in the front—ya know, hiding your face."

April cut her eyes back at him. "Whereas you hide your face with your pants."

Scott almost spat out his food laughing. "That's my girl."

Dakota walked up to the table beside May. Scott saw her sneak him a piece of sausage, and he held his head up, waiting for another. May looked at him for a moment before saying, "Speak."

"No," Scott said, but it was too late. Dakota barked and woke Joey up.

Joey started crying in Karen's arms. As she rocked him back and forth, May looked over at her, mouthing the word *sorry*.

She nodded that it was okay and started to sing to Joey. Her voice echoed softly in the room as Joey's crying lessened.

Scott listened to Karen's voice in amazement. It sounded so perfect. He watched as she rocked Joey back and forth, singing to him. They looked so beautiful together.

Finally, Joey's crying stopped, and he went back to sleep. Scott watched as Karen leaned down and kissed Joey's forehead.

As she looked back up, Scott smiled at her. "I've never heard you sing like that."

"What do you mean? I used to sing to April all the time when she was a baby."

"Not like that."

The clock hit 6:17. The kids got ready for school and lined up at the door. Scott watched as they ran out to the bus. Karen stood beside him, her arm around his waist.

"Why did you want to know the date?" Karen asked as the bus drove off.

"I was just curious, that's all."

"You don't have to tell me," she said, turning to face him. "Just don't pretend I don't know when something is bothering you."

"Deal," he said as he picked up his keys. "I'll see you tonight."

She winked at him as he left.

On his way to work, Scott dialed Dr. Freeman, hoping he would pick up, but once again, the call went to voicemail.

"Hey, this is Scott again. I left you a message yesterday and didn't know if you had heard it. No rush, just call me back when you can. Thanks."

Scott hung up the phone just as a crow crashed into the car windshield. Feathers flew everywhere as he slammed on the brakes. The crow sat on the hood, dazed for a moment, before flying away. Scott's eyes followed the crow as it took flight over the car and through the field. He struggled to catch his breath as he saw where it landed. On the scarecrow, surrounded by more of its kind.

There were at least a hundred of them scattered out over the field—perching on trees, flying in the sky, or resting on

the scarecrow. The crows bit into the scarecrow, ripping its overcoat more than it already was. The crow that had hit his car flew above the rest and rested on the rusted spike sticking out of the scarecrow's back. The crow screeched as it took its talons and reached down, scraping the scarecrow's face.

One crow burst out of the scarecrow's chest, followed by dozens more, crawling out of the hole, straw spilling everywhere. But there was something else on the straw. The straw was stained, glowing red from the sunlight. It was stained with blood.

Scott hit the gas and drove as fast as he could down the road. He was just seeing things again, he told himself. It wasn't possible. He drove all the way to work, never taking his foot off the gas.

Once at work, Scott rushed to the elevator, not stopping to talk to Ms. Betty. He walked in and pushed the button. The door closed, and he rode it up to his floor. Elevator music played in the background as he waited for the door to open up to his floor. Finally it did, and he walked straight to his office, locking the door behind him.

Scott paced as he tried to get the image out of his head, but it wouldn't go away. The black feathers, the bloodied straw, the horde of crows. It consumed his thoughts, until his phone rang.

He thought it must be Dr. Freeman, so he answered it immediately. "Hello, Doc?"

"Umm, is this Scott Murdock?"

The voice was unfamiliar to him. "Yes. May I ask who's calling?"

"Yes, this is Ryan. I'm calling from the county library to inform you of a late fee."

Scott thought for a minute before answering. "I haven't checked out any books from there. I haven't even heard of that library to be honest."

"Are you sure, sir? Our records show your name on file."

Suddenly he remembered April's school paper. He had assumed she had just gone to the school library. "Oh, yeah. My daughter could have checked out a book for school a few weeks ago. Mark Twain or something."

"What is your daughter's name?"

"April."

"I'm sorry, sir, that name isn't in our system. Also this book shows it was checked out a few days ago. It was signed for by a Scott Murdock."

"Can I ask the name of the book?"

"Let me see what I can do."

Scott paced the floor, half paying attention to the call.

"Are you still there, sir?"

"Yes."

"Okay, good. So the desk clerk remembers checking it out to you. It had a bright red cover and black lettering with a gold wrap. It was from the Devils and Witchcraft section, specifically titled *The Resurrection of Souls*."

Scott almost laughed over the phone in surprise. "Yeah, there is no way I checked that book out. You must have the wrong name or something."

"Okay, sir, thank you for your time."

"No problem." He hung up the phone and set it on his desk. He laughed for another second as he sat down in his

chair. The call had gotten his mind off the scarecrow, and he started back to work.

Scott sat at his desk for hours, going through paperwork, until he noticed a drop of blood on his desk. His arm was bleeding again, staining his shirtsleeve. He rolled it up and took his tie off to wrap around his arm to stop the bleeding.

Once it stopped completely, he got out his phone to call Dr. Reynolds. It rang for a second before he picked up.

"Hello?"

"Hey, man, this is Scott."

"Oh, Scott, hello. How are you holding up?" Dr. Reynolds asked.

"That's actually why I'm calling."

"Oh."

Scott leaned back in his chair. "Yeah, you see, my arm keeps bleeding."

Dr. Reynolds hesitated. "When you say bleeding...?"

Scott wasn't sure how to describe it himself but decided to try. "It bleeds down from my forearm, covering my hand. It looks like there may be a small cut, but not big enough to be bleeding this much."

"Hmm." Dr. Reynolds thought for a moment. "How much blood are you losing? Enough to make you feel lightheaded?"

"Not really."

"It's probably nothing, then. You could come in and I could look at it, but honestly, all I could really do is stitch it up for you."

"Okay, I was just going to check to make sure."

"Hey, if you're worried about it, just get Karen to sew it up for you. I'm sure she'd love the excuse to stab you with some needles."

Scott chuckled. "I'm sure she would."

"Anyway, if there's nothing else, I've got a surgery to get to."

"No, that was it. Take care, man." Scott hung up the phone. Despite his reassurances, something still felt off about his arm bleeding, but what could he do about it?

He was about to start going through more paperwork when he noticed blood had dripped on the brown envelope that Kyle had given him. He picked it up to wipe the blood off when he decided to go ahead and look at the numbers, not that he could actually do any of it.

Scott opened up the envelope and slid the papers out onto his desk. Only it wasn't numbers, or any kind of paperwork for that matter. It was police reports.

Scott stared down in horror at the files. He skimmed over them, not fully grasping what they were. They were from the incident when he was a child. He continued to flip through them, reading as he went. Certain words caught his eye. Scott Murdock, age eight. In isolation for seventy-three days. Found in a farmhouse. Scott started to read faster. Extremely malnourished. Fear of crows. Scar tissue covering his back. Birdcage. Blood found on hammer. Psychopathic tendencies. Immediate therapy recommended.

Scott set it down and covered his face with his hands. His heart pounded inside his chest as he struggled for air. He had begun sweating, causing the dry blood on his shirt to start dripping again. Then he saw something at the bottom of the files. A picture.

Scott moved the police files off to see it. He gagged into the wastebasket beside him when he saw the picture of the crime

scene. The bloodstained carpet, the police tape, and the body of the man who had kidnapped him.

Or at least what was left of it.

The memories all came flooding back to him at once. The mental pictures overwhelmed him. He shook his head back and forth, trying to think. This couldn't be happening. It was impossible. He looked back down at the police files on his desk. They couldn't be real. He was just seeing things, that's all it was. He hadn't slept in days, and he was just hallucinating.

But no matter how much Scott lied to himself, no matter how many times he turned away and looked back, those files still sat on his desk, along with the picture.

He grabbed them and threw them in the wastebasket beside him. He then grabbed a lighter from inside his desk and set it on fire.

The flames grew taller in front of his eyes, ashes floating up into the air in front of him. The fire consumed the files, and the picture with them.

How had they gotten into that envelope? Had Kyle put them there as some kind of sick prank? Had he just been hallucinating? Or was it something else?

Scott did know one thing, though. He couldn't stay at work.

He rushed out of his office and into the elevator. He didn't stop to talk to anyone. As the door opened, Scott stepped in. The door shut before anyone could join him, and the elevator began to drop.

As Scott stood, anxious for the elevator to reach his floor, he heard the sound playing from the speakers. Only it wasn't

elevator music. It was the scraping of claws. He panicked as he started to have flashbacks. Trapped in a small room, hearing the horrible sound echo of the walls. It seemed like an eternity before the door finally opened.

Scott practically ran out the front door, not stopping to answer Ms. Betty when she asked what was wrong. He raced across the parking lot to get into the car and drove off onto the blacktop road, trying to forget.

Later that day, the family was sitting down for dinner. Scott was in the kitchen, washing his hands, when he heard Karen say something.

"What?" he turned to ask.

Karen looked back at him from the dining table. "I didn't say anything."

"Oh," Scott said as he finished and walked over to the dinner table. He sat down, and the kids started to pass the food around.

They made small talk for a while, Karen asking the kids how their day was, Tommy and April joking with each other, until May asked Scott something. But he didn't hear her, his mind lost in thought about the police files.

"Huh?" he asked.

The whole family looked up at him. "We didn't say anything?" April said.

Scott looked at them for a moment. "Sorry, must've just heard something."

The kids had returned to small talk when it happened. All at once, he heard it. He looked up at his family, eating dinner

like every other night, exchanging small talk or talking about school, but he couldn't hear it. He watched their mouths move, but he didn't hear the words coming out. All he heard was the sounds of them crying.

Horrible, awful crying. Scott tried to say something, but he was in shock. He looked around at the kids, his head consumed by the sounds of their wailing. It was all he could hear. He tried to say something to them, but the words wouldn't come out. Then he saw Karen.

Karen was rocking Joey in her arms, singing to him, but all Scott heard was her bitter cries. Her cries were different from the kids': louder, full of anguish. He tried to call out to her. He tried to tell her it was okay, screaming at the top of his lungs, but his voice was consumed by the noise.

"Are you okay, Dad?" April asked, looking over at him.

The voices in Scott's head vanished as he looked over at his family, who were looking at him with concern. He was sweating in his chair and breathing heavily.

He took a moment to catch his breath before answering April. "I'm fine, honey. Just tired, I guess."

"Did you at least call Dr. Reynolds about the arm bleeding?" Karen asked from across the table.

"Yeah, he said it was probably nothing. Just to keep an eye on it, make sure it doesn't get worse."

The room sat quiet for a moment before Tommy broke the silence. "How was work?"

"Work's work," Scott said, trying to change the subject. "Oh, I almost forgot. Did anyone check out a book for school from the local library?"

"No, if the teachers give us a paper on something, it's always in the school library," Tommy answered, confused by the question.

Scott clarified. "I got a call from the library today and was just making sure."

"Oh," Tommy said. "Yeah, we didn't rent anything from there."

"What did you say the name was?" April asked, playing with the food on her plate.

"I think the guy on the phone called it the county library."

"Hmm," April said as she smiled to herself.

"What?" Scott asked.

"Oh, nothing. It's just, I used to like that place."

"You've been there before?" Scott asked, taking a bite of food.

"I used to go a lot."

"They have a good selection?" Karen asked.

"Yeah, you could find anything there if you looked hard enough."

Later that night, Scott was lying in bed, desperately trying to fall asleep. He tried to block the events of the day out of his mind as he closed his eyes, trying to drift off, but it was no use. He was wide awake.

He turned in the bed, looking up at the ceiling fan. He counted the spins it made, trying to distract himself long enough to fall asleep.

He had counted up to 342 when he heard May scream. The scream woke Karen, and they rushed to her room. Scott

walked down the hallway first, followed closely by Karen. They had just reached the door when they saw it was already open.

Scott peeked his head around the door, seeing April sitting inside on the bed, hugging May.

"She had a nightmare," April said to them as they walked in.

"Oh," Scott said as he kneeled down in front of May. He put his hand on her shoulder, causing her to jump.

"I can stay in here with her tonight," April offered.

"No, that's okay, honey," Scott said. "I'll stay."

"Are you sure?" Karen asked.

"Yeah, I got it. I couldn't sleep anyway."

April and Karen walked back to their rooms while Scott stayed with May. He sat on the bed beside her as he wiped a tear from her eye. "It's okay, nothing is going to hurt you." He put his hand on her back, feeling her shaking. "Do you want to talk about it?"

She shook her head no.

"Are you sure? Sometimes it helps."

She hesitated before speaking. "You were in it."

"I was?" he asked, surprised.

May nodded. "You walked into my room, but something was wrong. You acted scary."

"Scary how?"

May's voice cracked as she spoke. "You had scars on your face and you looked mean. You wanted to drown me in something. Something red."

"Oh, baby," Scott said as he hugged her. He looked down into her eyes, still filled with fear. "You know, your dad has

nightmares sometimes too," he said, trying to distract her from her own nightmare.

"Really?" she said as she looked up at him.

"Oh yeah, all the time," he said as he picked May up and sat her on his lap. "In fact, I always have the exact same one."

May stopped crying for a moment. Scott could tell he had gotten her attention. "What is it?" she asked.

"Well, there's a cage."

"Like the one we put Dakota in?" May's voice perked up.

"Kinda. Except in my dream, Dakota's not the one in the cage. I am."

May's eyes widened, and Scott smiled. He had managed to get her to stop shaking.

"So, I'm in the cage, all by myself, when I manage to open it and escape. It's too dark to see anything, so I just start running—until they show up in the darkness. I can see their eyes looking at me and hear their horrible cry as they scrape their claws against the ground." Scott's mind had gotten lost in the thoughts, not noticing May starting to shake again. "Then they all head straight for me as I cry out for help, but no one answers. I just have to watch them come after me one by one."

"What are they?" May asked, terrified.

Scott looked down, realizing he was scaring her. He thought for a moment. "Unicorns."

She looked at him, shocked. "You're scared of unicorns?"

"Oh, terrified," he said. "The bright colors, the magic wings, the horn. It's the stuff of nightmares."

May started giggling.

"What, you don't think unicorns are scary?"

"Uh-uh," she said, shaking her head.

"Wow," he said in disbelief. "What a brave girl."

She laughed at him as he tucked her back into bed.

"I guess I'm not so scary now."

"No," May said, still grinning ear to ear.

"How about I read you a story before I go?" Scott said, grabbing a book from the shelf beside him at random. He looked at it in his hands and smiled when he saw which one it was. *Cat in the Hat*. He opened it up to the first page, seeing the engraving Dr. Freeman had left when he'd given it to them. He hesitated for a moment as a feeling of remorse spread over him. He brushed it off and began reading it to May.

Once he finished, Scott leaned down and kissed her on the forehead. "Goodnight, baby." He turned around and opened the door but stopped and whispered back to her, "Let's keep the unicorn story between us." He gave her a wink, which she returned. "That's my girl," he said, shutting the door behind him.

Scott walked back to his bedroom, feeling the soft shag carpet beneath his feet. Karen had already fallen back asleep in the bed. Lucky.

He then walked into the bathroom to splash water on his face. He shut the door but left the light off. As the cold water ran down his face, he looked up into the mirror and saw something. The cut he had seen on his cheek was back, but it wasn't the only one.

Deep cuts covered parts of his face. He ran his hand over his face, not feeling any of the horrific scars he saw in the

mirror. When he reached over to turn the light on, the cuts vanished. His reflection was normal again.

Scott let out a sigh of relief. He reached to grab the door handle but turned back, noticing something behind him. His heart pounded in his chest, his lungs froze up, and chills went down his spine. The white porcelain bathtub was covered in blood.

"This isn't real," Scott said as he stared in horror. Blood was everywhere, staining the tub, pouring down the drain. But it wasn't just on the tub. It covered the walls too. Crimson blood was splattered everywhere, sinking down from the walls in twisted streams. It poured down into the tub, filling it up faster than the drain could release it.

The blood started pouring over the tub, spilling onto the floor, soaking into the tile. It reached Scott's feet as he stood frozen in fear. But it wasn't the blood that scared him. It was the note.

Scott stepped towards the bathtub, his eyes fixed on it. A single green Post-it note stuck to the wall, not stained by the blood. Two words had been scribbled onto it, but Scott was too far to read it. He continued to move closer until he reached the edge of the bathtub. As his hand hit the wall, warm blood cascaded down it.

He stretched his hand out toward the note, his heart sinking in horror as he made out the words that were scribbled on it. His lungs spasmed, robbing him of air. "No, no, no," he pleaded as he stared at it.

He told himself that this was just a hallucination. That he would close his eyes and it would all disappear like some sort

of bad dream. So Scott closed his eyes, just like he had done when he was a boy trapped in that cage, and he waited. Waited until it would go away. Until everything would be okay. Until he would be safe again.

To his surprise, when he opened his eyes, the blood was actually gone. Not a trace was left anywhere, the bathroom returning to its perfectly white interior. The blood-soaked tile was clean, and even the blood on Scott's hand had vanished. But the note was still there.

As were the words scribbled on it.

Scott's knees buckled at the sight of it. It was real. He fell to the floor, leaning against the wall. His mind panicked. It was impossible. Dr. Freeman had said it was impossible.

Scott struggled to get his phone out as horrible flashbacks kept entering his mind. He dialed Dr. Freeman, begging that he would pick up, but it went straight to voicemail. He tried calling again.

"It's Scott, please pick up." Scott waited, hoping, praying that he would pick up, but no answer came. "Please, Doc, I need your help. I think the crash did something to my head, and I've been hallucinating, and just—just, please pick up. I think—" Scott choked as he looked over at the note and the words written on it. *Not Alone.*

"I think—I think he's back."

Chapter Six

Day 42

Scott felt helpless in the field as the crows dove straight for him. It seemed like thousands of them, covering the sky in a blanket of darkness. The sun shined through the ridges of their black feathers, casting twisted shadows on the ground. They screeched out in unison and in an instant, they were on him.

Dozens of them flew around Scott, circling him like a shark, scratching him as they went, their sharp talons tearing into the scars on his back. He tried to look up, but all he could see was black feathers streaking by as he felt more of their long claws digging into his skin, opening up his flesh.

Their screeching was all-consuming. Their cries multiplied around him, filling his ears with the horrific sound. He didn't know what to do. He couldn't run, he couldn't fight. All he could do was scream out for help. Then, as he began screaming, his head started to hurt.

The man heard Scott's screams and ran up to him, shooing the crows back. He threw Scott across the field, right into the scarecrow.

Scott crashed into the scarecrow, crying out in pain, when his head twisted violently. Something was happening.

The man walked over to him, whip in hand. "After all I did, you try to run away," he shouted as he cracked the whip on the boy's back. It tore into the already open wounds, and it felt like fire spreading over his spine.

Scott felt his hand twitching. His head started to shake more violently as a sharp pain, not caused by the whip, shot through it. It felt different than anything he had felt before, and he screamed out from the pain.

The man watched the boy, confused by his screaming. He hadn't cracked him again with the whip, and yet the boy's screams were louder than before. He watched as Scott's entire body started twitching badly. The screaming stopped for a moment before starting back. Then the cycle repeated again. The screaming was erratic, one moment bloodcurdling, the next complete silence.

Scott was experiencing pain like he had never felt. His head felt like it was going to explode. He couldn't control the twitch any more than he could control the pain. His vision wavered. One moment he saw the bloodstained grass below him perfectly clearly, and the next moment all he could see was darkness.

The man took a step back, unnerved. He had never seen anything like this. The unnatural twitching, the twisting of limbs, the horrific screaming. It was like something out

of a horror movie. Only he was watching it with his own eyes.

The screaming only grew louder. Before long it was loud enough to cause the crows to fly away completely, as fast as they could. They flew past the man, all the way back to the tree in the distance. Scott's body continued to distort as he let out one final scream, more bloodcurdling than any that had come before, and then sat in complete silence as everything went black.

The man watched Scott as he sat in the field, his body no longer shaking, other than his hand, which twitched slightly. The expression on the boy's face caused the man to step back slightly. His eyes seemed to be filled with rage, and yet somehow looked calm. Unsettlingly calm. The man looked down at him, thinking he was a fool to be afraid. The man tried to rationalize it. It must've just been a seizure or something. Yeah, that was it. The boy had just had a seizure. The only problem with his theory was that he wasn't looking at Scott anymore. In fact, Scott wasn't there at all.

It was something else.

It looked down at the ground, trying to figure out where It was. It saw the grass underneath It, covered in Its own blood. It saw the crow feathers littered around It in the field, and the scratches on Its arm, where the crows had scraped Scott. It saw the crows watching from the trees. It looked back to see the scarecrow sitting behind It. It tilted Its head as It looked for a moment, before It felt the whip crack against Its back.

The man was surprised. The boy didn't scream out in pain. The force from the whip knocked the boy down, but It stayed

quiet, not making a sound. The man cracked the whip once more, but still the boy just flinched, taking the pain in silence.

It looked back up at the man. It wanted nothing more than to take the whip from his hands, to crack it against his skin. Make his flesh tear away from his body, spilling his blood onto the grass. Hear the man scream in agony as his life was stripped away from him inch by inch.

But It had lost too much blood. It could barely stand up, and when It did, the man's whip pushed It back down to the ground. It could already feel Itself losing consciousness as the man continued to beat It with the whip, pain surging through Its entire body. It sat silently in the field as It blacked out.

Day 43

Scott woke up in the cage. The lock was back, and his food and water had been taken away. Heat was coming in through the window.

He raised himself up as much as the cage would allow and rested his back against the bars. His mind was foggy. The last thing he remembered was the crows tearing into him, and then his head hurting. He tried to think. The man was there, beating him, and then—he couldn't remember past that.

The hot metal of the bars singed his back, but his skin had gotten used to it by now. It just singed over the scars that were already there.

He didn't try to open the cage door. He didn't even check to see if the lock was still on it. He was trapped in the cage, and

he decided he needed to accept that. If he went out again, the creatures would still be there, waiting for him.

Scott rested his eyes as the sun went down in the sky. The crows had returned to the roof, scraping their talons against it, but it wasn't enough to keep him awake. Not tonight. Not when he'd lost so much blood.

Not when It wanted out.

Day 44

It woke up.

It looked around, surveying the room, paying attention to the details. The light shining through the single window. The tools hanging up on the walls. The small size of the room. It stopped looking at the room and began to inspect the cage. It had thick metal bars, rusty but strong enough to keep It in. It leaned forward and pushed the door when It saw the lock. A padlock, three inches long, and too thick to be broken.

It looked back into the room. Glass was still scattered over the floor from when the crow had burst through the window. It reached out to grab a piece.

If It could grab a piece, It thought, It could use it to kill the man when he came back. It would wait until he leaned down by the cage and slit his throat, but at just the right angle to make it slow. Watch him bleed out onto the floor, long enough to realize that he was dead, lying in a pool of his own blood. But then It wouldn't have the key and would be stuck there.

But that didn't matter. It couldn't reach the glass. It would have to find another way. It surveyed the room further, looking for anything at all, but found nothing of use. At least not as long as It was still in the cage.

It looked at the bars on the cage, where Scott had made notches to keep track of how many days it had been. It lifted up Its fingernail and scratched another notch into the rust.

Night came. It leaned back in the cage, watching as the moonlight slipped through the window. It had closed Its eyes to sleep when It heard it for the first time. The crows flying to the roof, the sound of their talons echoing off the walls.

It watched the window as a crow flew down from the roof, landing on the windowsill. It tilted Its head slightly to watch the crow, which did the same to watch It. It looked at the crow's features, its sharp claws, its dark eyes. But most importantly, its long black feathers.

It sat back in the cage as the crow flew away. It sat motionless, staring into the distance, thinking of a way out. A way to escape. A way to kill.

Day 45

Scott sat in the cage, his stomach crying out for food. It had been days, and the man hadn't so much as stepped in with a drop of water. His entire body ached from dehydration. He barely had the strength to sit up in the cage.

Bloodstains lay scattered across the floor, stretching out to almost where the broken glass was. He tried to think.

He didn't remember reaching his arm out to try and grab a piece.

He sat hunched over in the cage, trying to figure out what was happening, when he saw the mark on the cage. One extra day had been added. A notch that Scott hadn't carved. A day he didn't remember.

Day 46

It sat in the cage, still without food or water. Its tongue was like sandpaper in Its mouth as It lay balled up, barely holding on to consciousness. Then the rain started to pour down.

The sound of the rain on the shed rung through Its ears as It lay on the floor. The wind blew hard against the rain, blowing it into the shed. The water started to fill up into a puddle, right on the edge of Its cage.

It leaned Its head over, licking the water off the dirt-covered floor. The rain water was cold and brought It back from the brink of death. It laid Its head down in the water, trying to cool off from the intense heat as It waited for night to come.

It could feel something in the back of Its mind. Something else was there. Someone else. It tried to focus on it, figure out who or what it was. But all It could make out was that the other thing, whatever it was, was scared.

Day 51

Scott watched as the door handle twisted and light poured in through the door. The man stepped in, carrying a bottle of water and a dog pail. He walked over to the cage, kneeling down by Scott. He sucked his teeth slightly as he looked in at him. "I suppose you've learned your lesson about running off."

Scott nodded his head, not stopping to think. He didn't care that the man had him locked in a cage. He was too scared to ever run again, and he needed water.

"Good bird," the man said as he poured a little water into the pail and placed it into the cage for him to drink. As he leaned over to drink it, the man slammed his hand against the metal bars, causing him to jump back.

"You've learned when I say you've learned." The man picked up his whip and proceeded to beat him with it.

As the man walked out of the shed, Scott lay on the floor in a pool of his own blood. He could feel himself dying. He wanted to. There was no point in living like this. He couldn't run, he couldn't eat. At least if he died, he wouldn't hurt anymore.

Then he saw it. Something had been scraped on the rusted bars. Something Scott didn't remember writing. Two words carved into the rust.

Not Alone.

Day 56

It looked at the bowl of birdseed in front of It. The man had finally brought it in, thinking that the boy might die soon without food. But the food came with a price, lashes all across Its back and arms.

It leaned down to take a bite of bird food. It tasted rancid in Its mouth, but it filled Its stomach. It finished almost all of it, saving a little for what It had to do at night.

Night came, and the crows returned. It took the seed in Its hands and tossed it up onto the window. Some landed on the windowsill—not very much, but enough. A crow flew down from the roof and landed on it, pecking the seeds. It tossed more up to the crow as more joined in eating, the moon resting in the sky behind them.

Day 65

Scott felt his back. A new set of fresh scars that he didn't remember getting, and more notches on the bars, an extra one every day he looked at it.

The moonlight shined through the window, illuminating the creatures standing on it, as many as could fit on the windowsill.

Scott jumped back in the cage in horror as they began to screech at him, their screeches mixing with the scraping of the other creatures still on the roof. He listened in terror, balled

up in the cage, waiting for daylight to come. Scott never fell asleep.

Day 66

Scott was still awake when morning came. The creatures had stayed all night, crying out to him. He was shaking with fear as he looked over at the markings on the bars. There wasn't another one. Whatever he felt in the back of his head hadn't come out. Not when he hadn't fallen asleep.

Day 69

It threw the birdseed up to the windowsill and the crows flocked to it. It waited for them to finish and be hungry enough to want more. It threw some more to them, but this time on the floor beneath the windowsill. It waited patiently for them to fly down, but only one did.

The crow landed on the floor in front of It, pecking at the birdseed until it was all gone. It watched the crow and threw a little more, right in front of the cage. The crow stepped towards the food.

It watched, waiting for it to get close enough. Just a few more steps and—

The crow lifted up its jagged wings, flying up to the ceiling and making its way out of the window, back into the night sky.

It leaned back, resting on the bars of the cage. It was so close. Just a few more days, and the crow would be close enough.

Its hand began twitching as It fell asleep dreaming about it. Longing for it. Escaping and finding the man. Taking his life. Watching him lie on the floor dead, in a river of his own blood.

Day 72

Scott didn't bother raising himself up in the cage. What was the point? He was never going to escape. All that was waiting for him on the other side of the door was the winged black creatures. Scott couldn't bear the thought of them coming after him again, crawling over his skin, clawing into his flesh with their talons.

He listened to them at night, moving above his head, and his mind flashed back to the field. He remembered them tearing into his skin, opening up his wounds. Flying around him like a swarm. Screeching in his ear, drowning out his cries for help.

Even sleep didn't save him from them. They haunted his nightmares just the same. Every night, he dreamt of being locked in the cage with them as their black eyes watched him through the darkness.

But Scott could feel someone else in his head. Something else. Something twisted.

Day 73

It waited for night to come. The moonlight began shining through the window. Within moments, they were there. The crows.

It tossed food up to them, watching them peck it off the windowsill. It then threw some on the floor. This time, several were brave enough, or hungry enough, to fly down. It tossed some closer and watched the crows walk towards it.

Their talons dragged on the ground as they walked. Their wings were folded back into their side, and their heads lowered to the ground, looking cautiously. Two crows fell back, but one continued on.

It watched the crow. Just a little closer. Just a little closer and it would be enough. It continued watching as the crow inched its way closer, eating the seeds as it walked. Just a step farther and, there—

It grabbed the crow in Its hand. The crow cried out in pain, struggling to escape Its grip. The crow's wings beat against the air, trying to fly away, but it couldn't. Then, its cries were silenced, and its wings went limp.

It had broken the crow's neck and dropped it to the ground. It reached down to rip out one of its feathers—one from its wings, longer and sturdier. It tossed the crow to the side and reached Its hands through the bar.

It reached to the lock, turning it as best It could to get the right angle. It shoved the coarse black feather inside it and listened carefully. It moved the feather back and forth,

listening for the sound of gears turning. It was hard to hear over the sound of the crows on the roof, scraping in panic due to the dead crow's cry for help.

There it was. The lock opened up. It pulled the lock off the cage and pushed the door open, stepping out. It stayed expressionless and walked to the wall of tools.

First was the saw. The saw was two feet long, and the metal was rusty and jagged. Good for torture, It thought. But It would have to kill him fast, or the man would have enough time to react, and then It couldn't savor the death as long.

Second was a drill. The drill bit was a circular drilling blade, three inches long and twisted. It examined the drill but moved on. Too unpredictable. If the drill ran out of battery before It was done with the man, he might be able to fight back.

Third was a hammer. About a foot long, with a wooden handle. It examined the hammer, thinking it over. The blunt side could hit the man in the temple, causing enough pain to immobilize him, but not kill him, so that he could still feel the pain. Then It could turn the hammer around in Its hand, to the sharp, curved side, and make the death last a very long time.

It reached up and grabbed the hammer from the shelf. The hammer felt heavy in Its hand as It walked to the door. The door was locked, but the handle was cheaply made. One swing of the hammer and It broke off the door, causing the door to swing open.

It stepped outside, walking across the yard. The moon was just bright enough to illuminate the crows, who watched

It walk towards the house. Some flew at It, scraping Its arm, but It didn't flinch.

It reached the house and opened the door. As It walked in, It heard the answering machine playing in the background. A man's voice came out from the speaker.

"Pick up the phone," the man on the machine said, forcefully and with a British accent. "Pick up the phone now. You've missed your last four sessions. I know what you've done. I've seen the news."

It paid no attention to the answering machine as It walked into the living room, seeing the man passed out on the couch, drink in hand.

"I know you've kidnapped that boy. Pick up the phone, or I will call the cops right now, I swear." The man on the phone was yelling now, and the voice message could be heard all the way to the living room, but the man on the couch didn't wake up.

It walked over to the man on the couch, staring at him for a moment. Its right hand was shaking violently as It waited to do it. It could already feel it. The sound of the man screaming. The warm blood covering Its hands as It took the man's life from him. It breathed in deeply as Its hand became perfectly still. It raised the hammer up and poked the man on the shoulder, watching his eyes open.

It wanted him to be awake for this.

Day 74

The sun was coming up over the field as the cops pulled up to the house. They stepped out onto the grass, and walked

toward the front door. Crows watched them walk from the roof of the house.

"Police, open up," they shouted as they banged on the door, but no answer came. After a few moments, they broke down the door and stepped in. The cops walked down the hallway with their guns drawn.

As they stepped around the corner, they saw the remains of the body lying on the living room floor.

Dr. Freeman arrived right after the cops. He stepped out of his car, wearing a dark brown trench coat. A brown hat sat atop his greasy black hair as he made his way to the house. The cops tried to caution him.

"I'm his psychiatrist," he proclaimed as he walked past the cops into the house. He turned the corner and saw the body of his patient. He barely kept from vomiting. Some of the cops hadn't been so lucky.

Dr. Freeman knelt down, taking his hat off, trying not to look directly at the man. "I'm sorry I couldn't help you," he said with pain in his voice. "I tried." He stood to face the cops.

"Who was he?" the officer in charge asked.

Dr. Freeman said plainly, "A patient of mine. Over a dozen mental disorders. I tried to help him, but over the last few months I could feel him slipping. I had no idea it had gotten this far until I saw the news of a boy missing." Dr. Freeman looked down at the body for a moment, immediately regretting it. "Have you found the boy?"

As he asked the question, a cop came from the next room, his face pale. "Sir," he said as he looked down at the floor, spooked.

Dr. Freeman followed the officer in charge to the next room. As he walked, he saw a trail of blood leading in. In the middle of the floor sat a hammer, soaked in red. Dr. Freeman was almost afraid to look up from the floor at what the officers were walking toward, but he forced himself to. He cut his eyes up from the hammer to the boy sitting in the corner of the room.

"We found him," he heard the lead officer say over the intercom as he looked at the boy. Thin as a bone, his ribs showing through his stomach. The boy's face was drained of color, no doubt from malnutrition. As Dr. Freeman walked closer, his stomach churned. He tried to hide the fear in his eyes as he looked at the boy, curled up in the corner, drenched in blood.

Blood that wasn't his own.

Chapter Seven

Morning came, and Karen walked into the bathroom, only to see Scott sitting on the floor, staring at the wall.

She rushed over to him. "What's wrong?"

Scott looked at her, his eyes filled with fear. "He's back." He repeated it more forcefully. "Karen, he's back."

"Who's back?" she asked with a confused expression. He turned his head, looking into her eyes, and she realized. "Oh."

He nodded, and they sat silently for a minute, processing it.

She shook her head. "No, that's impossible, Dr. Freeman told you it was impossible."

Scott simply pointed up at the note stuck to the wall. She turned her head to look at it, gasping in shock. She walked over to it and pulled it from the wall, staring at it, trying to think. "When did you find this?"

"Last night," he said . "It was there when I got back from May's room."

"It wasn't there when we went to bed," Karen stammered, looking for an explanation. "When could 'he' have put it there?"

"I don't know."

"You have to remember something," she said. "When could he have come out?"

"I said I don't know!" Scott shouted, frustrated, before immediately backtracking. "I'm sorry, honey, I didn't mean to—it's just... I didn't fall asleep last night, and I certainly didn't black out. I remember the entire night. I have no idea when he could have come out."

"Okay," she said plainly. "If you didn't fall asleep, then this couldn't have been him. There has to be another explanation." She walked over to Scott on the floor and sat down beside him. "There has to be."

He could hear the pain in her voice. "You're probably right." He reached over and took her hand. "But if he is back somehow—"

"Don't," Karen cut him off midsentence, her eyes watering.

Scott nodded. "Okay."

They both remained on the floor, looking at the wall, trying not to think about what had happened so many years ago.

Later that morning, the kids had almost finished eating breakfast. Scott had just a few bites of eggs and a sip of coffee left when the kids started getting ready for school. They took their plates to the kitchen.

When Scott was done, he walked into the kitchen to wash his plate. Karen was standing by the refrigerator, holding Joey in her arms. Scott heard crying and looked down at Dakota's dog bowl. He realized Dakota hadn't come in for breakfast this morning, and then he heard May's crying voice from outside.

"Wake up."

He turned to look for her, noticing the kids weren't in the kitchen anymore but the back door was open. "Where'd they go?" he asked Karen.

"Backyard," she said. "May wanted to say goodbye to Dakota before school."

Scott walked to the window to look out at them in the backyard and heard May's voice again, breaking up from tears. "Please wake up." He saw her out the window, hunched down over Dakota, who was lying flat in the grass, not moving.

Scott motioned for Karen to come, then walked out the back door onto the grass.

April and Tommy stood behind May, holding their hands on her back as she still pleaded to Dakota. "Please wake up." She reached down and shook him.

Scott walked up behind her, looking down at Dakota. He saw the glazed-over look in his eyes, and the tongue hanging out from his mouth.

"Please wake up. Please, Da—"

April cut her off. "It's okay," she said as she pulled her back and hugged her. "It's going to be okay."

"Why won't he wake up?" May asked, crying in April's arms.

Tommy leaned down beside May. "Maybe he will. Maybe he's just waiting for you to go hide so he can come find you, like when you used to play hide-and-seek."

That made May finally stop crying.

Scott leaned down to look at Dakota. He reached over and shut his eyes, then rubbed his hand across his back. His fur felt cold to the touch. No one said anything for

a few minutes, until finally April asked, "What do you think happened?"

Scott looked down at Dakota, seemingly peaceful as he lay in the grass. "Probably old age. We got him almost nine years ago. His breed doesn't live much longer than that, and he'd gotten sick last summer. Maybe it came back."

May started to cry again, and Scott put his hand on her shoulder. "Don't worry, sweetie. He was probably dreaming about you."

May stopped crying. "Really?"

"Of course," Karen added. "He was probably dreaming of playing fetch."

May wiped the tears off her face as Scott looked at his watch. 6:17.

"Are you okay to go to school?" Karen asked May, who nodded. "Okay, then, go get ready."

Tommy lifted May up onto his shoulders, trying to cheer her up. "Come on, I'll give you a ride into the house."

They all walked back into the house and got ready for school. As they were grabbing their backpacks, Scott walked up to April. "Tonight is when you have the parent-teacher conference after school, right?"

"Yeah," she said as she slung the backpack over her shoulder. "But Mom already said she could go, so you're off the hook."

"You sure?" he asked as he looked over at Karen. "I don't mind."

"Yeah, I got it," Karen said as she rocked Joey back and forth in her arms. "I have to take Joey to the pediatrician for a checkup anyway, so I'll just swing by there afterwards."

"I thought you took Joey for his checkup last month."

"No," she said as she looked up at Scott.

"Are you sure?" Scott asked, confused. "I could've sworn you said you were going to town to take him last month."

"I'm positive," Karen said defensively.

"Okay," Scott said as he walked toward the kids at the door. "Must've just misheard you."

"Wouldn't be the first time," she joked as she walked up beside him.

April opened the door for Tommy and May. Scott could feel the cold air coming in as he watched them walk to the edge of the porch and step off towards the bus.

It started to rain on them. It was barely more than a sprinkle, but enough to get them wet. The rain hit their hair and dripped down onto their faces before starting to come down harder.

The rain was pouring down now, drenching their clothes. It made a thunderous noise as it fell out of the sky, covering everything in sight. The kids had almost made it to the bus when they turned around to wave goodbye, rain still pouring on them. Only Scott didn't see rain falling from the sky. He saw blood.

Thick red blood pouring down from the clouds, drenching his children as they walked to the bus. He watched in horror as they turned around to wave, unaware of the blood that covered them, streaming down their faces, soaking their hair.

May waved as Scott stood paralyzed. He didn't know what to do. His mind told him to scream for them, to run out and save them from it, but his body wouldn't move.

"Scott?"

The blood was pouring down even harder now. Scott could barely see his kids through it. April turned to get on the bus, followed by the others. Then the rain grew silent as he heard it. The scraping. The digging of claws through metal. He looked up to where a single crow perched, digging its talons into the top of the bus. Its feathers weren't stained by the blood, remaining completely black. The crow watched the kids get on the bus; its head tilted sideways.

"Scott?"

The clock rang out beside him. He turned to look at it, seeing the time flashing on and off. The time that the clock was stuck on. 6:17.

Scott turned back to see the kids as the bus began to drive off. He tried to fight his body, to run out to help them, to save them from the crow, but he stayed still, paralyzed with fear.

"Scott?" Karen said, her voice snapping him out of it. "What's wrong?"

Scott looked at her, seeing her concerned expression. He turned back to the window, seeing the bus drive down the street. The rain was normal, not a drop of red anywhere to be seen, and the crow was no longer perched on top of the bus, or anywhere else in sight.

Scott breathed a sigh of relief and turned back to Karen.

"Is something wrong?" she asked again.

"No, it's just—" His voice cut off. He didn't know what to say. "I think I'm going to take the day off from work."

"That's a good idea," she said. "Especially considering."

Scott saw in her eyes what she was thinking about: the message left upstairs.

"I know," he answered.

Karen kissed him on the cheek and walked back through the living room. He went to follow her when he noticed the clock. It was still stuck on the same time. 6:17. Scott looked at it for a moment before reaching over and unplugging it.

Later that day, Scott grabbed a shovel from the garage. Its handle was wooden, but its blade was sharp metal, though slightly rusted. Scott picked it up and carried it through the house and out the back door.

The rain had disappeared now as he stepped into the backyard. The grass was still wet, and the sky was dark and gray. The air was cold as he walked over to Dakota's body. Scott knelt down beside him, rubbing his hand across Dakota's back. "You were a good dog."

Scott stood up and began digging a hole in the edge of the yard. It was next to the only tree in the backyard, an old oak. He pushed the shovel into the ground, starting a grave.

The grave was dug underneath the tree, with Scott standing in the shade of its branches. He was about three feet down when Karen walked out to him, holding Joey in one arm and a bottle of water in the other. She tossed him the water as she looked down into the hole, seeing the loose soil within it.

Scott nodded thanks and drank the water, setting the empty bottle on the grass beside him. Karen looked at him, rocking Joey in her arms. "I'm about to head out to Joey's checkup. Need anything before I go?"

"No, I'm good. Just going to finish digging."

"Alright, then, I'll see you tonight after April's teacher conference. I'm going to catch a ride with Susan, so the car will be here if you need it."

Susan was their next-door neighbor. "Sounds good," he said as Karen walked back to the house. She turned to wave goodbye at the door before walking in.

Scott returned to digging the grave.

After almost an hour, he finished it. Five and a half feet down, wide enough on either side for Dakota to lie in. Scott put down the shovel and walked over to Dakota.

Dakota lay lifeless on his side in the grass as Scott rubbed his back. He knew he couldn't feel it, but it felt right to do it anyway. He continued to rub his back, with his hand sliding over Dakota's dark black fur. He planned on waiting for May to get home to bury him, so he started to stand up, when he noticed the sun shining off something in the grass beneath Dakota.

Scott leaned down to look at it. A small red stain on the blade of grass, reflecting light from the sun. He reached his hand down to touch it and the red crept onto his fingers. Blood.

He looked down at Dakota, lying on his side dead, and flipped him over, seeing that it wasn't old age that had killed him. The grass where he had lain was stained with blood, Scott realized as he examined the other side of Dakota's body. The side covered with cuts.

The cuts littered the body from head to toe, dozens of them scattered out, some deep, some shallow. Scott stepped back in horror as he looked at them. They horribly disfigured that side of Dakota, to the point of making him unrecognizable.

"No," he said to himself as he looked at the body. His mind raced. When could this have happened? He had been awake the whole night, and then with Karen that morning. He hadn't even seen Dakota until May had found him dead. "He" couldn't have done it, Scott thought. It was impossible.

His mind continued to race. What if it was who Scott thought it was? What if "he" really was back? A chill went down his spine as he thought of it. *No, that can't be it. "He" can't be back.* He was just hallucinating from no sleep, he told himself. *That's it.* But deep down, he knew it wasn't true. This wasn't a hallucination, and neither was the Post-it note in the bathroom. Karen had seen it too. It was real. Just like the message written on it.

The words rang in Scott's head. *Not Alone.*

Dakota's gruesome body still lay in the grass. He knew he had to bury it now. He picked him up in his arms, blood spilling onto his shirt, and carried him to the grave. He set him in it gently and picked up the shovel.

"I'm sorry," Scott said as he started to cover him up with dirt, filling the grave back up with cold dark soil. His voice was breaking up as he said his final words to Dakota. "Goodbye."

Scott paced the living room. The ceiling fan above him made a creaking noise as it spun around slowly. Behind him was the wall with family pictures on it. His head was filled with terrible thoughts. He kept watching his phone, praying that Dr. Freeman would call him back. He needed someone to talk to about this.

He knew he could talk to Karen, but it was different. She didn't understand the same way. Felt differently. Didn't see the

monster. Maybe she was right. No, he couldn't think like that, especially now. She just didn't realize what it felt like. What "he" thought of. Dreamed of. If she'd known, she would have understood, he was sure of it.

The phone never rang. He continued to pace the floor until his eyes caught a picture on the wall, a picture of May on her first birthday, when they had gotten her Dakota. He was just a puppy then, but her eyes had lit up when she had seen him. Dakota had licked her face the moment he'd seen her, and they had been best friends ever since. But she wasn't the only one who'd loved Dakota. Scott remembered when April had had nightmares after the incident, and how Dakota would sleep in her room at night to make her feel safe. Or when Tommy would take him to the dog park so Dakota would have a wide-open space to run in. Or when Joey was born, and Dakota had immediately decided it was his job to watch over him. That was only a few months before he had gotten lost.

Scott remembered how heartbroken May had been. Karen thought he must've slipped through a broken board in the fence and gotten lost, but Scott had always had a different theory. Dakota was getting older by the day and had been sick for a while. Scott always thought he had slipped through the fence on purpose, to find a spot to die. Dogs did that sometimes, and it made sense. Part of him wished it had been true.

But then Dakota had shown back up, only to die like this only a few days later. It wasn't right. He deserved better. But thinking about Dakota had gotten Scott's mind off the message left upstairs. He smiled. Dakota was always good when it came

to that. Distracting you from whatever was wrong at the time, making you feel better.

Scott looked at the time. It was getting pretty close to when Tommy and May would come home from school. He turned back, noticing the pictures on the wall. He looked over them, realizing the picture of Joey at the hospital the day he was born still wasn't hanging up. As a matter of fact, no picture of Joey was hanging up.

April must've put them somewhere, Scott thought as he looked around the living room for them. He looked through the pictures on the bookshelf and below the seats, just in case. Then he remembered the drawer at the bottom of the end table in the corner on the room. The kids would always put stuff in it, and he had even stored things in it from time to time. *That's probably where she put the pictures of Joey*, he thought as he walked over to it. It was made from wood, and its handle was made from a dark brown metal and stuck out from the drawer about an inch.

Scott reached and opened the drawer, taken aback by what he saw. There were no pictures, or anything else that the kids normally put in it. Inside, a single item lay diagonal, taking up almost the whole length. A kitchen knife.

Its handle was black, with two silver screws in it. Its blade was nine inches long, made out of stainless steel, sharpened precisely across the edge. The steel was bright silver, but the edge was stained with blood. Dakota's blood.

Scott slammed the drawer shut. It couldn't be real. It couldn't be. Not that knife. He reopened the drawer, seeing the knife still sitting in it, stained in red.

It couldn't be the same one, Scott thought to himself. It couldn't be; he had gotten rid of it years ago.

Scott pulled out his phone, calling Dr. Freeman, but still no answer. He hung up in frustration and slammed the drawer shut with the knife still inside it when suddenly he heard the door open. He turned to see Tommy and May walking in, setting their backpacks on the couch.

"You okay, Dad?" Tommy asked. "You look a little rough."

"I'm fine," Scott said as he looked back down at the closed drawer. "Just tired."

"If you say so," Tommy said as he picked up May, carrying her around the living room on his back.

Scott thought for a moment. He had to get help, to figure out what was happening. It was too dangerous for him to stay here without knowing for sure if "he" was back. Scott walked over and put on his coat. "I have to go," he told Tommy. "Can you watch May until I get home?"

"Sure," Tommy said as he set May back on the floor. "Where are you going?"

"Nowhere important," Scott lied as he picked up keys to the car. "Just someone I need to talk to. I should be back within an hour."

"Okay," Tommy said as May ran across the floor to Scott.

Scott knelt down to hug her. "Bye, honey."

"Bye, Dad."

As Scott walked to the car, he looked back to see Tommy playing with May through the window. The air was cold, and it had started to mist again when he stepped into the car. He looked back at the kids one more time before driving off, heading straight for Dr. Freeman's office.

Chapter Eight

Scott drove down the blacktop road, never slowing down. He had to talk to Dr. Freeman. He would know what to do, Scott thought. All he had to do was talk to him. Figure out what was going on, and if "he" really was back, they would just have to do it again. What they had done so many years ago. What Scott still carried guilt for. But it had to be done, he told himself. The safety of his family was more important.

He sped down the country road, not stopping for anything. The sky was gray, and rain was trickling down from the sky. The air was cold, cold enough for him to feel it from inside the car.

The side of the road was littered with trees, but Scott didn't pay any attention to them, except for the old cedar tree. His heart dropped in his chest when he passed by it, seeing the dirt torn up in the ditch where his car had peeled off the road. The bark was scraped off the tree where the car had crashed into it.

The crash must've given him head trauma, Scott thought. *That's how "he" is back.* It had messed up something in his head, brought him back out. But when could "he" have done

these things? "He" would've had to come out several times, and yet Scott hadn't fallen asleep, blacked out, or so much as had a headache. "He" couldn't be back, Scott decided. It wasn't possible. There had to be another explanation. Dr. Freeman would find it.

As he drove down the road, he came to the field. He glanced over at it, not wanting to look. The wind was blowing the rain as it came down in the field, pounding into the soil. The dead brown wheat was being blown sideways by the wind, and Scott could hear it rustling from inside the car.

Scott forced himself to look closer into the field, afraid of what he might see. But when he looked, he realized it was gone. The scarecrow that had sat in the field had vanished. The field sat empty, barren, without a single thing in it, but above it, they flew through the air.

Crows, watching him from the sky. They scattered in the air, rain beating down on their wings. There were too many to count, streaks of black twisting in the air. Their wings seemed massive as they flapped them in the air, flying further into the sky, hidden in the clouds, where he could no longer see them.

Scott put his foot on the gas, driving straight to the therapist's office. He had to get help, he thought. Dr. Freeman would help him. He would understand.

Scott pulled up to the therapist's office. It was a small building, the outside of which was brick. It was rented out by multiple therapists in the area, just big enough for all of them to have separate offices. He walked across the gravel parking lot and up to the door.

He looked at his watch: 7:15 p.m. The other therapists in the building would have gone home by now, but he knew Dr. Freeman. He always stayed late, working on patients' files, trying to figure out how to help them. Scott felt grateful. It used to be his files that Dr. Freeman would pore over late into the night, trying to help Scott. Trying to help both of them.

But some people couldn't be helped, he thought as he stepped in. Just like the man who had kidnapped him. Dr. Freeman had thought he was helping him, making a difference, but eventually the man couldn't resist the temptation. The urge. All it took was a single moment, and all the good Dr. Freeman had done him was washed away. Undone.

Scott walked through the door and past the receptionist desk. The receptionist chair was empty. *Probably just went home when the rest of the therapists did*, Scott thought. Dr. Freeman would never make anyone wait on him to leave.

Scott walked down the empty hallway towards Dr. Freeman's office. It was across from the corner, at the end of the hallway. The doors on either side were shut, and the lights that hung from the ceiling were turned on but were dim and flickering. One second the hallway would be lit up, and the next darkness. The hallway echoed with the sound of the flickering lightbulbs, ringing in his ears.

Now at the end of the hallway, Scott turned toward Dr. Freeman's door. It was the fifth one down, at the very end of the hall. He stepped toward it as the sound of the lights flickering went away, replaced by complete silence. Only the sound of his footsteps on the hall carpet could be heard as he approached the door.

The door was cracked open. The light inside was on, but much dimmer than normal, barely showing up in the crack of the doorway. As he pushed the door open, the light inside the room started to flicker and went dark for a moment. He took one step into the room, everything still quiet. Suddenly, the light flickered back on, illuminating the room.

Scott stared in horror at the scarecrow in the middle of the floor.

It was propped up on a stake, which stuck out its back. Its arms were tied to the side, stretched out in a T position. Its head hung down from the stake, limp from its body.

A hole was carved out of its chest where the crows had clawed their way out. Coarse black feathers still remained in the cavity.

Its dark brown overcoat was torn to shreds on its body. Ripped pieces of it hung down by threads from it, stained in red. Atop its head sat a brown hat, hiding its face. Scott's eyes widened as he recognized it.

He stepped toward the scarecrow, hesitating. Blood stained the granite floor, splattered around the room, leading back to the scarecrow. Blood dripped down from its body, pouring onto the floor beneath it.

Scott stepped in it as he continued to walk towards the scarecrow. The light was now flickering violently as he continued walking.

The stench almost gagged him. The scarecrow gave off the smell of rotting flesh as he tried not to breathe it in. He was only a few steps away when he heard it.

Sccrrreeee

Scott couldn't see where it was coming from as the sound echoed off the walls. It consumed the room, drowning out the sound of the light flickering. The horrible scraping. His neck twisted sideways at the sound of it.

His mind desperately told him to run away, to run out the door and never come back. Run away from the sound of the crow, away from the vile stench, away from the scarecrow in the middle of the room. But he had to know. He had to see it with his own eyes, to know it was true. That it wasn't just another nightmare that kept him up at night. It wasn't just some sleep-deprived hallucination caused by the crash. It wasn't just the flickering light playing tricks on him. Scott had to know if "he" was really back.

Scott stood right in front of the scarecrow. A chill went down his spine as he reached for the scarecrow's thick brown hat. He lifted it off his head slowly and saw the face underneath. The face of the man he had known since he was a boy. The face of the man who had tried so desperately to help him. Dr. Freeman.

The hat dropped out of his hand onto the floor as he stepped back in disbelief. Scott couldn't breathe as he looked at Dr. Freeman, impaled on his own rusted metal coatrack, dressed like a scarecrow.

Dr. Freeman's face had been drained of all color. His skin was white as a sheet. The decay had started to set in, his skin withering away, his face now resembling a skull. His eyes had rolled back in his head, now milky white and lifeless. His mouth hung open, his teeth having fallen down to the floor as blood dripped from his now hollow mouth.

It was all Scott could do not to scream. He stood frozen in fear, looking at the scarecrow, as his mind raced. Why would "he" do this? Dr. Freeman had always tried to help "him" even more so than Scott. Except for—

Scott's breath choked at the thought. If "he" had done this to Dr. Freeman, Scott was next. The moment he had always feared was here, and there would be no running from it.

Scott stood there, his mind telling him to run, but his body wouldn't listen. He couldn't move as he stared at Dr. Freeman's rotting corpse. Then, he heard it. The sound of talons scraping. His gaze moved from the corpse to the desk in the corner of the room. A single crow sat atop it, digging its talons into the wood, tearing it open. Wood splintered over the desk as the crow tilted its head sideways, watching him with its dead eyes.

The crow flew from the desk onto Dr. Freeman and dug its claws into his shoulder. It turned its head and started pecking on the side of Dr. Freeman's face, its sharp beak tearing through what little flesh was left.

Scott stepped back toward the door before he saw something on the floor. Dr. Freeman's notepad. Its old yellow pages crunched as he picked it up, and he stared in horror at the word Dr. Freeman had scribbled on it violently, probably as he was being killed. His heart dropped in his chest as he looked at it, a word he hadn't spoken in years. A name.

VINCENT

Scott stepped back, closer to the door. He looked down from the ceiling back to the crow perched on the scarecrow's shoulder. As he stepped backwards out the door, the crow raised its wings, spreading them out on either side. Screeching, it lifted itself into the air, flying toward him.

Scott ran through the hallway as the flickering light hid the crow from view. It beat its wings, following him. As he reached the corner, he almost ran into the wall as he turned to run out the door. The light was flickering off more than on now as the crow appeared behind him in fleeting glances before being hidden again in the darkness.

Scott reached the door and pushed his way out it, slamming it back before the crow could get out. The crow sprawled its wings out, stopping itself just short of the glass door. It then sat on the floor, watching him.

Scott kept his eye on the crow behind the door as he backed up across the parking lot. The only sound that could be heard was his own shoes walking on the gravel. As he stepped back from the building, he took his eyes off the crow and saw what was on the roof of the building.

Crows covered it, thousands of them spreading out over every inch, staring down at him. He began walking faster to his car, now only a few yards away, when, without making a sound, the crows dove for him. Scott turned around and ran to his car, slamming the door shut, as hordes of them beat against it, blocking out the sun.

Scott started his car, but it didn't deter them. They flew around it, frenzied. Scratching the glass. Clawing the metal. Trapping him inside. He slammed on the gas and drove

through them as fast as he could. Finally, after almost two dozen yards, they stopped and flew back up into the sky.

Inside the car, Scott was panicking. What if they came back? Or, worse, what if they followed him home? What if they didn't stop coming for him? But the thought of Dr. Freeman's body haunted him more than the crows.

How could he be dead? What would Scott do without him? How would he handle what was happening?

Scott's mind drifted to the name. Could it really be him? Was it possible? And if it was, if Vincent was really back, what was he going to do?

Chapter Nine

It had taken him a few weeks, but Dr. Freeman had finally convinced the boy's parents to let him be his psychiatrist. He didn't blame them for being hesitant, especially since his last patient was the reason the boy had been taken in the first place. But Dr. Freeman knew that he could help this boy. He needed to help this boy and atone for his part in this, his failing with the captor. And he would help this time, he decided, no matter what it took.

Dr. Freeman sat in his office as he waited for them to arrive. He had set out a fresh plate of donuts in case the boy was hungry. Food always made patients more comfortable, and while he had never had a child patient before, he was sure it helped them all the same.

He walked over to his coffee machine in the corner of the room, pouring himself a cup. The steam rose up from it as the smell of coffee entered the room.

A coatrack sat in the corner of the room. It was metal, and very tall, almost reaching the ceiling. Its hooks stretched out to the side, holding Dr. Freeman's light brown hat. He thought

it impolite to wear the hat while meeting the parents in person for the first time.

Dr. Freeman checked his watch. It was almost time for them to arrive. He waited patiently in his chair until he heard a knock on the door. He set his cup of coffee down and walked over to the door, opening it. Outside the door stood the parents, both of whom looked tired and worried, and in the middle stood the boy, a scared expression on his face.

"Nice to finally meet face-to-face," Dr. Freeman said as he pointed down the hall. "If you don't mind, I'd prefer to talk to you two before I speak with your son. He can wait in the room at the end of the hall."

"Of course," the mother said. She walked Scott to the room before returning.

Dr. Freeman motioned them into his office, and they all walked in and took their seats.

"Coffee?" Dr. Freeman offered, gesturing towards the machine.

"No, thank you."

"Okay, let's get right to it, then." Dr. Freeman pulled out his notepad and rested it on his crossed legs. "I've seen the police reports, and I've looked over all of the evidence they have."

The mother cut him off right there. "Scott didn't kill that man, Doctor. Our son doesn't have it in him to do something that cruel."

The father continued her point. "Now, we're not saying the man didn't deserve what he got, just that our son couldn't have been the one to do it. Our son is a good person, and he went through a lot, yes. But to do something like the police claim he did, something that inhuman, it's just not our son."

Dr. Freeman was shocked by their boldness, but at least they were being honest with him. "Well, if my theory is correct, it may not have been your son, but time will tell. Either way, the police won't be giving you trouble. It was clearly self-defense."

"But Scott didn't do it," the mother repeated. "I don't like the police or anyone else claiming he did something that atrocious."

Dr. Freeman squinted at her, in disbelief that she would object to the mere suggestion her son had killed someone in self-defense, but chose not to push her on it. "Okay, then, let's move on to my next question. How has Scott been behaving these past few weeks?"

The father thought for a moment before answering. "Different."

"Different how?"

"Well"—the father paused—"it's hard to explain. Some days he acts like you would expect him to, a frightened little kid who just went through something horrible. He cries in his sleep, has nightmares. Trouble eating. But some days—"

The mother joined in. "Some days he's different. Doesn't really talk at all. Doesn't seem scared. Almost calm."

Dr. Freeman wrote that down on his notepad. His assumption was looking to be right, which meant the boy had a difficult road ahead of him, one that he himself wouldn't wish on anyone, especially an eight-year-old boy.

He finished writing his notes and then stood up. "I think I have enough to go on. I will speak with the boy now." He reached out his hand, shaking theirs. "I will do whatever I can to help him."

The parents nodded and walked out of the room to get their son.

Dr. Freeman took out his notepad as Scott sat down on the couch, not saying a word.

Dr. Freeman examined him a moment before speaking. The boy was sitting slumped over, shaking slightly with fear. He still hadn't gained back the weight he had lost from the months of isolation, and he sat staring off into the distance.

"My name is Dr. Freeman. May I ask what yours is?" He knew Scott's name, but he thought the question might put the boy at ease.

"Scott," Scott said, finally looking at him.

"It's nice to meet you, Scott. Do you know why you are here?"

"My parents said you're a therapist, and that you would help me feel better."

"Well, not exactly." Dr. Freeman paused before continuing. He wanted to make his intentions clear. "I'm not like a normal doctor that you come to when you feel physically sick. I'm more for when you experience mental trauma." He could see that Scott was having trouble understanding, so he tried to clarify. "When you're afraid of something, or when you feel something is wrong with your head, I try to help you understand what it is, so that it's not as scary."

Scott nodded.

"I would like to start by asking you a few questions. Is that alright?"

"Yes, sir."

"Have you had any nightmares recently?"

Scott nodded and shifted uncomfortably on the couch.

"Can you describe one for me?"

Scott started shaking worse. "It's always the same. I'm in the birdcage, and then the creatures come for me."

"I see." Dr. Freeman was concerned about him referring to the crows as creatures but didn't want to bring it up just yet. "Do you ever escape the cage?"

"Yes. But they follow me out. They attack me whenever I escape. Hundreds of them." He continued to shake.

"That must be terrifying," Dr. Freeman said, trying to comfort him. "But you know, recurring dreams are pretty common for someone who experienced what you did. It's perfectly normal to be afraid, but the nightmares can be a good thing."

"How?" Scott asked, confused.

"Nightmares are a sign that your mind isn't ready to let go of what happened yet. That's the good part. Since we know what is causing them, we can deal with it directly."

"How do we deal with it?" he asked.

"Therapy," Dr. Freeman said, half-joking.

Scott laughed for the first time in months.

Dr. Freeman looked at him. It was the first time since he had come in that the boy wasn't shaking. Dr. Freeman examined his actions as the boy caught his breath. He could tell the boy was scared and didn't know how to deal with it. He was going to help him; he just had to figure out how.

"Why do you think you dream of these 'creatures'?"

"They were there when I was in the cage," Scott said, his laughter turning back to fear in an instant. "They walked on the roof at night, trying to get in."

"They ever attack you?"

Scott nodded. "The cage was unlocked, so I tried to run. I made it to the field when they found me." His voice grew louder as he spoke. "I tried to get away, but they were all over me. They hurt me."

"What happened then?" Dr. Freeman could tell Scott was upset, but he needed to know.

"The man found me. He beat me. I tried to get away, but my head started to hurt, so I blacked out. I don't remember anything after that."

That's it, Dr. Freeman thought. That was the moment it happened. The moment Scott's mind couldn't take it anymore. The moment of stress so great his mind had split. The moment something else had arrived.

Dr. Freeman was scribbling notes when Scott started talking again. "Why did he do it? Why did he take me?" His voice was breaking up with the sound of him crying now. "Why did the creatures attack me? I didn't do anything to them."

"Oh, son," Dr. Freeman said as he got up and walked over to the couch beside him. "It was nothing that you did."

"Then why?" Scott pleaded.

Dr. Freeman sighed. He had hoped to avoid telling Scott this but decided he needed to hear it. "The man that abducted you was a former patient of mine."

"Really?" Scott asked, rubbing his eyes.

"Yes, he was, and he was very sick. He had a tendency to torture things. He knew it was wrong but couldn't stop himself. It started when he was younger. He would step on insects and

things like that. Normal child stuff. But soon he started to kill bigger things. Like birds."

"What happened?"

"I was making real progress with him. He had stopped hurting things, and I thought he was getting well. But then a crow flew in front of his car. It was injured and was suffering, so he put it out of its misery. He told me he was fine, that everything was okay. I had no idea how far it had gotten." Dr. Freeman stopped and looked down at Scott, shaking beside him. "The crows that attacked you were there because he lured them there. He was setting out birdseed for them and then taking some into his house, to torture."

Scott looked up at Dr. Freeman with wide eyes. He couldn't believe the evil man had been killing the crows.

"You see, Scott, the crows were prisoners there just like you were. They just attacked you out of fear. It's all they knew how to do."

"Was the man going to kill me?" Scott was afraid to ask but couldn't help it.

Dr. Freeman looked at him with sympathy. He hated to tell him, but therapy only worked if they both told the truth. "Yes. You see, Scott, that's the thing about a mental illness. No matter how hard you work, one incident, like the crow hitting his car, can undo all the progress you've made. And once you go back downhill, there is no stopping it."

"Will that happen to me?" Scott asked, scared.

"Of course not," Dr. Freeman declared. "You are not the same man he was. You have different problems."

"Promise?"

Dr. Freeman stood up and walked back over to his chair. "Promise." He jotted down some more notes while Scott sat quietly on the couch. "Feel free to take a donut."

"Thank you, sir, but I ate before we came here."

"Well, if you change your mind." He finished scribbling notes and thought to himself. He needed to know more about Scott's blackout. "When the man was beating you, you said you blacked out. Has that happened again?" He was surprised when Scott shook his head no. That put a dent in his theory. Unless... "You said you have nightmares every night, correct?"

"Yes?" Scott said, not fully understanding the point of the question.

"What happens after them? Do you just wake up the next morning?"

Scott hung his head down. He had hoped he wouldn't ask that.

"You don't, do you?"

"No."

That was it, Dr. Freeman thought. That was how the other personality was coming out. "When you go to sleep, you don't wake up the next morning, do you? You wake up the morning after that."

Scott nodded as his eyes watered. "I'm sorry."

"It's nothing to be sorry for, Scott. Nothing at all. But tell me, do you remember anything from the days where you don't wake up?"

Scott shook his head. "Bits and pieces, but not very much."

Dr. Freeman wrote that down. It was normal for personalities to have a certain level of awareness, even when the other had control. "Does he leave you messages?"

Scott looked straight up at him, surprised by the question. He wasn't expecting Dr. Freeman to know so soon. "Yes."

"What kind?"

Scott hesitated, not wanting to get in trouble.

"You can tell me," Dr. Freeman reassured him.

"He leaves me messages on Post-it notes."

"Are they threats?"

"No, no," Scott said, not wanting Dr. Freeman to misunderstand. "It's just normal stuff, I guess. Questions and things like that."

"Do you respond?"

Scott shook his head no. "I'm afraid to, I guess."

"You should," Dr. Freeman said. "Couldn't hurt."

"Okay."

They stayed quiet for a moment as Dr. Freeman thought of how to ask his next question. Was it even possible? Maybe they could only switch by falling asleep. But it was worth a shot. "Can I speak with him?"

Scott didn't know what to say. "I don't know if I can change. It usually only happens after I go to sleep. I never forced it to happen."

"Can you try?" Dr. Freeman asked.

Scott nodded his head and closed his eyes, but he wasn't able to.

"Try to remember how you felt when you switched the first time."

Scott kept trying, imagining himself back in the field, surrounded by the creatures, until finally his head started to hurt.

He grunted in pain and leaned over in his chair. He held his face with his hands as his right hand started to twitch violently. He screamed out in pain before becoming completely silent.

Dr. Freeman watched, knowing what was now sitting on the couch wasn't Scott. It was something else. It sat perfectly calm, staring at the floor. The only movement It made was the slight twitching of Its right hand as It continued to stare at the floor.

Dr. Freeman considered saying something but thought it best to stay silent. After a few seconds, Dr. Freeman lost his breath when It looked up from the floor, straight at him. Its expression was unnerving. Its eyes lit up with anger and pain, but Its expression remained calm.

Dr. Freeman caught his breath as he looked back at It for a moment. Then It closed its eyes, and Scott came back.

"Did it work?"

Dr. Freeman struggled to collect himself after witnessing it. So young and yet so full of hurt. Born into a bird's cage, being beaten by a stranger. Trapped in a shed. It looked worse than he had ever imagined. "Yes. Yes, it did."

Scott waited in the hallway while Dr. Freeman talked with his parents.

"Is he okay?" the mother asked.

"Your son is going to be fine," Dr. Freeman replied.

"Did he kill that man like the police say?"

"No, ma'am. Rest assured 'Scott' didn't kill anyone," Dr. Freeman said. "But it's a little more complicated than that."

"Complicated how?" the father asked sternly.

"Your son suffers from DID, Dissociative Identity Disorder."

"Which is?"

Dr. Freeman sensed hostility in the father's voice but chose not to address it. "Put simply, the stress your son was under caused a fragmenting of his mind, another personality if you will. Your son didn't kill his captor, but the other personality did."

"Okay," the mother said. "How does Scott get rid of it?"

Dr. Freeman was appalled by the question. "How does Scott get 'rid' of it?" he repeated, almost mocking.

"Yes, what does Scott have to do to get rid of the other 'thing' or whatever it's called?" The mother's tone was forceful, seemingly put out that she had to repeat herself.

Dr. Freeman looked at her with shock. He couldn't believe her response. "You call it what it is. Another person, a child who, by the way, saved your son's life."

"Spare me your philosophical opinions, Doctor. That thing killed a man, and I need to know how Scott makes it go away."

Dr. Freeman looked at her in disgust. How could someone be so immediately cruel and coldhearted? It was almost as if they thought the mere fact that it wasn't their son condemned it to death. Dr. Freeman replied, trying to bite his tongue. "Scott can't get rid of it. One personality can't kill another. If they could, then that particular field of psychiatry wouldn't really be necessary, now would it?" He couldn't help sounding a little sarcastic.

"But *you* can," the father stated. "You can get rid of it, right?"

"Theoretically, yes—"

"Then do it," the mother pronounced.

"No," Dr. Freeman said simply.

"Why not?" the father asked. "We'll pay for whatever the procedure costs."

Dr. Freeman just stared at them, his mouth almost open. "It's not a question of money. It's a matter of killing an innocent boy who has done nothing wrong."

"Nothing wrong?" the father asked, confused. "That thing killed a man."

Dr. Freeman's tone grew louder. "Yes, a man who kidnapped your son and caused the mental split. And had the other personality not killed him, the man would've killed both of them."

"But the things it did to the man. It's not human."

"This is not a discussion," Dr. Freeman stated. "The other personality may be sick, disturbed even, but considering the conditions he appeared in, I would say he deserves a chance to get well before we give him the death penalty."

"Fine, but if it hurts anyone, it's on your head," the father said, pointing at him.

"Very well."

The parents left the room and walked down the hallway. Dr. Freeman took one last look at Scott before shutting his office door.

Dr. Freeman thought about Scott. He was just a scared little boy, not understanding why such a thing had happened to him. The nightmares of being in a cage were normal and should subside given enough time and therapy. But there was something else that haunted Dr. Freeman's thoughts. The other personality.

He had only seen it for a moment, but it was like nothing he'd seen before. The pain in its eyes was excruciating, and yet its expression was completely calm. Unnervingly calm.

He had to help him too, Dr. Freeman decided. He couldn't have another patient lose their soul to their own demons. Couldn't have more blood on his hands. Not when it was a boy. Not when it was his fault that it existed.

He would help him. He would look past the sickness, past the signs that he was beyond saving, and try to help him. He owed him that much.

Chapter Ten

Scott pulled up in his driveway. The sun had set in the sky, being replaced by moonlight. It shone down from the sky, pouring through cracks in the clouds. The rain had stopped, and instead there was a fog so thick he could barely see his house in front of him.

Scott noticed that the neighbor's car wasn't in the driveway. Karen must not be home from April's school conference. Good, he thought. He needed time to figure out what to say.

No light was on in the house, save for a single flickering light shining through an upstairs window. He approached the door, watching his back for the crows, but they hadn't followed him.

As Scott reached for the doorknob, he hesitated. How could he go into his house, be around his family, if he couldn't trust himself? If there was even the slightest chance that Vincent was back, how could he take that risk?

His grip loosened on the doorknob for an instant before tightening back. He had to go in, he decided. He had to be

with his family. Running away wasn't the answer. He turned the doorknob and walked inside.

Inside, the house was different. The pictures on the wall sat crooked while others had fallen, the glass shattered across the floor. The fan remained on the ceiling, creaking as its blades spun slowly. The furniture sat slightly askew.

Scott stepped through it, seeing the drawer in the corner of the room. The drawer that now sat half-open. He stepped over to it, his feet crunching the broken glass beneath them. He didn't want to look inside the drawer, didn't want to see what he had left there, but he had no choice. He opened the drawer the rest of the way and forced himself to look inside.

It was empty.

No, no, no, he thought. This wasn't happening. How could the knife be gone? Who would have known to look there? Who would've taken it? The only one at the house was—

Scott's stomach churned at the thought. No, they couldn't have found it. But what if they had? What if they now knew the monster he was? The monster that Vincent was?

Scott dragged his feet back from the drawer, not wanting to accept it, when he heard something. A scratching.

It was coming from upstairs. The sound of claws scraping against wood echoed down the stairs, filling his ears with dread. Scott started toward the stairs, despite his mind telling him to run.

He had to see it with his own eyes.

He walked up the stairs as the clawing continued. With each step he took, the instinct to run grew stronger. What if it was a crow? What if it had gotten in his house? He could

just turn and run down the stairs, back into the night, but the crows would be there too. No matter where he ran, they would find him. They always found him.

Scott reached the top of the stairs and looked down the hall. Bedroom doors were lined up down the wall, each being closed. But Scott could see light seeping through the bottom of one, the one on the end of the hallway. May's room.

Scott walked over to it as the light flickered on the floor. The scratching had only grown louder, consuming the hallway with its twisted sound.

He approached the door, but how could he open it? How could he face the crow inside the room? The monster that waited for him on the other side of the door. The thing that haunted his nightmares from the first night in the cage. The creature.

Scott sat frozen at the door. He couldn't do it. His hand wouldn't turn the knob. He couldn't face what was inside. He took one step back from the door, turning slightly on his heel to walk away, when the door cracked open.

It made a creaking noise on its hinges, as it seemed to open itself, revealing what was inside. Revealing who was inside.

Scott stopped in his tracks. No, it couldn't be. His mind told him to run, but he stepped inside the room. The light flickered on the ceiling, illuminating everything.

Scott looked in horror at the words carved into the walls.

Sins of the Father

They covered every inch of the room, carved into the wood. Scott closed his eyes for a moment, telling himself it would go away, but it didn't. *Sins of the Father* was etched into

everything, the letters distorted and twisting. But that wasn't what scared him. It was who was carving them.

Tommy sat in the corner on the room, digging into the wall with his hand. His fingernails were bleeding as they clawed the letters into the wood.

Scott's heart sank. It wasn't him who was sick. It was Tommy. No, it couldn't be, he told himself. Not his son. He didn't deserve to go through that, to go through what he had gone through. Not like this.

"Tommy," Scott whispered as he walked up behind him.

Tommy didn't respond, instead continuing to scrape his hand down the wall, blood pouring out from his fingers.

"Tommy," Scott shouted as he grabbed his shoulder and spun him around. Tommy's eyes were black and lifeless, but only for a moment before returning to their normal shade of blue.

Scott shook him slightly, trying to snap him out of it.

Tommy shook his head back and forth as if realizing where he was. He looked up, still dazed. "Dad?"

"What happened?" Scott pleaded. He already knew the answer, but he couldn't accept it. Not like this. Not when it was his son. "What happened?" he repeated.

Tommy seemed to snap back to his senses as he looked at Scott, confused. "I don't know. I was downstairs with May, and then I must've passed out. I had this awful dream, and—" He stopped talking as he saw the scratches on the wall. "Who did that?"

Scott looked at him, seeing the fear in his son's eyes. "You did."

"What? No," Tommy said, shaking it off. "This wasn't me, I was just dreaming about it."

"What else did you dream?" Scott's tone was forceful. He had to know.

"I dreamt I was carving this," Tommy said as he reached his right hand up, feeling the words carved into the wall. "And then—" He looked up at Scott, his mouth open. "Oh no."

"What?" Scott said as he looked at Tommy, noticing his other hand for the first time, and the knife in it.

Tommy looked down at the knife, confused. He hadn't realized he'd been holding it. He hadn't even seen this knife before. But Scott had.

Scott forced himself to look at the knife as his heart broke. It was the knife that Vincent had used so many years ago, and now his son was holding it, and it was covered in blood, along with Tommy's hand.

"What did you do?" Scott screamed. "What did you do!?"

Before he could answer, Scott heard a faint cry come from across the room. It came from May's bed, underneath her sheets. Tommy dropped the knife from his hands as Scott rushed to the bed.

It had blood splattered on it, the sheets domed over in the center, with something lying underneath them. Something that was moving.

Scott pulled the sheet down slowly, revealing what was buried underneath. Lying there, with blood dripping from her mouth, was May.

Her pink dress was ripped to shreds, revealing the bloody flesh underneath. Stabs wounds littered her chest as she

coughed, her mouth filling up with the blood. She began twitching violently in the bed as she struggled to scream.

She was dying.

Tears fell down from Scott's eyes as he looked at her. He lifted her up in his arms and began carrying her out of the room.

Tommy started to follow when Scott turned back around. "No," he said forcefully. "You stay here."

"But I didn't—" Tommy said, almost crying.

"No! You have to stay here. I can't trust what you'll do."

With that, Scott left Tommy standing in the room, surrounded by the wicked carvings, as he ran down the stairs, holding May in his arms. He ran straight to his car and threw the door open, laying her on the passenger side.

May was still trying to talk as she faded in and out of consciousness, mumbling words Scott couldn't understand as he drove down the road toward the hospital.

Scott pulled out his phone, calling Karen. It went to voicemail.

"Karen, I need you to take April and meet me at the hospital. Don't go home, you hear me? Do not go home!" Scott's voice cracked as he spoke. "Something happened."

Chapter Eleven

Scott rushed into the hospital, carrying May in his arms. He ran straight past the desk to Dr. Reynolds, who was in the hallway, speaking to another patient.

"Doc," he screamed as he ran down the hallway.

"Scott, what brings—" His words were cut short when he turned to see Scott holding a bleeding May in his arms. He hesitated for a moment out of shock before taking command. "Lay her on that bed," he said, pointing at a white bed sitting across the hallway, next to a portable IV station.

Scott laid her down and Dr. Reynolds began pushing the cart toward the surgery area.

"What happened?" Dr. Reynolds asked as they ran down the hallway.

"She was stabbed," Scott said, not telling him how.

Dr. Reynolds shouted out orders to passing doctors as they all rushed to the operating room.

Once they reached it, the nurses picked May up from the bed and laid her on the operating table while Dr. Reynolds inspected the wounds. "We have multiple lacerations on the

chest and abdomen. The bleeding from the mouth indicates a ruptured lung."

The doctors inspected her for a moment before asking Scott to leave the room. Despite his objections, he was escorted out as the doctors began pulling out surgical tools and prepping her. This was going to be a delicate procedure, and they didn't have much time.

Scott stayed just outside the room for a moment, looking in through the large window used for when new doctors would observe surgeries, when Karen approached him from behind, seeing May bleeding on the table.

"No," Karen said, crying, as she fought to go into the room, being held back by Scott. She fought his grip, but he didn't let her go in, despite her screams of anguish for her daughter.

"We can't," he said as he held her back from the door. "We can't."

She stopped fighting him as a nurse approached the window, shutting the curtain on the other side. They were about to start surgery, and the parents shouldn't have to see it.

As they both looked helplessly at the now blocked window, Karen cried in Scott's arms.

April was in the waiting room, taking care of Joey, when Scott and Karen walked in.

"What's happening?" she asked as she leapt up from her chair to walk over to them. "Where is she?"

"She's in surgery," Scott said, trying not to show how afraid he was. She didn't need to see him afraid, not at a time like this. Not after all she'd gone through. "They said it could take a few hours."

As he said the words, April hugged him, holding him tight. "Dad, I'm scared."

"I know, honey," he whispered as he held her back, not being able to lie to her. "I am too."

They sat in the waiting room for what felt like days. It was a large room, with dozens of chairs lined up on either side, but it was mostly empty. Only a few people walked in and out, most of them nurses or staff. No one that came in made a sound, and the room remained silent, except for the sound of Joey crying. The walls were pale and gray, with little color in the whole room except a few old magazines scattered on the tables.

Scott sat next to April, who had rested her head on his shoulders. Tears streamed down her face, falling onto him. He moved his hand across her back, holding on to her.

In the next chair sat Karen, trying to keep Joey from crying. She bounced him up and down and patted his back, but nothing worked.

"Please stop crying," she said as she tried rocking him, but it didn't work. he continued to cry, no matter what she did.

She looked over at Scott as tears welled up in her eyes. "He won't stop crying. How do I get him to stop crying?"

Scott's heart broke as he saw her expression. The fear that was in her eyes. The fear that May wouldn't make it. He motioned for April to take Joey as he stood up and walked to Karen.

"He won't stop crying," she repeated as he held her. "Why won't he stop crying?"

"Oh, baby," he said as he fought back the tears himself. "It's going to be okay."

"Won't stop crying," she repeated as she tried to pull away, back to Joey.

Scott continued to hold her despite her pulling away. "It's okay." He tried to think of what to say to comfort her, but he couldn't find the words. He could tell her heart was breaking at the thought of May, at the thought of something happening to her, especially after what had happened to April. Karen couldn't take much more pain.

"It's okay," he repeated as she stopped fighting him. "It's okay."

Karen broke down, weeping in his arms.

"He won't stop crying."

Dr. Reynolds walked into the waiting room. Joey had long since calmed down, now asleep in Karen's arms. Scott stood up from his chair to meet him across the room. "How is she?" he begged desperately.

Before the doctor could answer, Karen and April also rose from their seats. "Is she alive?" Karen asked, her voice cracking.

"Yes," Dr. Reynolds said. "Her condition is severe and she lost a lot of blood, but she is stable for now."

"Can we see her?" April asked. "Please?"

"Yes, but only for a moment. We can't move her, so she will have to stay in the operating room overnight."

"Why?" Karen asked. "Could something still go wrong?"

"No, she is stable, but the lacerations on her chest ruptured her right lung, causing blood to spill into it. We have her

hooked up to a machine that siphons the blood out from her lungs, allowing her to breathe. But it can't be moved into a normal room, in case something did happen. We should be able to take her off it by tomorrow morning, but we'll have to wait and see how she recovers."

Dr. Reynolds began walking them toward the room, stopping outside the glass window. "Your little girl is strong," he told them. "Most people wouldn't have been able to pull through something like this, much less someone her age." As he grabbed the door handle, he looked at Scott. "Your guardian angel must be looking after her too."

Inside, Scott saw May lying in a hospital bed, with bandages wrapped around her chest. A small needle was resting in her arm for her IV, and a larger one rested in her chest, pumping out the blood as needed. Her bright blond hair was stained with red, but her eyes seemed full of life. She giggled when she saw them walking in the room.

Karen rushed to the bed, hugging May a little too tight.

"Oww," May whispered.

"Sorry, baby," Karen said as she let go.

"That's okay, Mom," May said, bubbly.

April was next over, looking at May smiling in the bed.

"April!" May said, excited, as she opened her arms for a hug.

April leaned down, hugging May gently. "Hey," she said softly. "How do you feel?"

"Good," May laughed as she pointed to the IV in her arm. "That tickles."

April turned back to the doctor, surprised, as he mouthed "pain medicine."

April let out a small chuckle as she stood back up, allowing Scott to see May.

"How's it going, sweetie?" he asked as he knelt down beside her bed.

She smiled at the question and reached over to the bedside table to grab a picture she had drawn.

"One of the nurses gave her crayons to draw with," Dr. Reynolds clarified.

She pulled up the picture to show Scott. It was a poorly drawn picture of a green field, with a pink unicorn running through the middle of it. She held it up close to Scott's face. "Boo."

Scott couldn't help but laugh. He laughed so hard that May began laughing with him as Karen and April looked at them with confusion.

"That's my brave girl," Scott said once he finished laughing. He leaned over and kissed her on the forehead.

Dr. Reynolds motioned that it was time to go. They all said goodbye to May one last time before walking out. Scott stayed a second longer, pausing to wink at her. May winked back, and Scott shut the door behind him.

Outside, Dr. Reynolds spoke with them. "You can go home for the night if you wish. I will make sure that she is well looked after."

"Thank you, but I can't leave her here alone," Karen said. "I'll stay the night."

"Very well," Dr. Reynolds said, walking away. "Let me know if you need anything."

Once the doctor left, Karen looked back inside the window at May, who had already fallen asleep. "Who did this?" she whispered to Scott.

He motioned his head towards the waiting room. They walked to it, and he pointed for April to sit down. "Watch Joey, I have to speak your mom about something."

"Is it about May? I want to know what happened too."

"No," he stated. "Right now you need to look after your brother."

"I deserve to know what happened," she proclaimed as Karen handed Joey to her.

"I understand, April, and you will. But first, I have to talk to your mother. Privately," he added when he saw she was about to say something.

Scott hated not telling April. She deserved the truth, not just about May, but about everything. She deserved to know after all these years, but he couldn't bear to tell her. She had been through so much, he didn't want to add to it. She shouldn't have to carry his burdens as well. Or his guilt.

Scott walked Karen to an empty hospital room, shutting the door behind him. The room was small, lit up by a single lightbulb in the ceiling. A bed sat in the corner, with a pull-out curtain hanging up beside it. A sink sat on the adjacent wall, dripping water out slowly.

"Who did this?" Karen demanded. "Was it Vincent?"

Scott didn't answer. How could he? He didn't want to accept it himself. He couldn't imagine how to tell her about Tommy. About what he had become.

"Was it Vincent?" Karen repeated, her tone forceful. "Did you talk to Dr. Freeman? Did he say anything about whether or not he could come back?"

"Dr. Freeman's dead."

"What?" she said, taking a step back in shock. "No, he can't be. How?"

"I found the kitchen knife in the house."

"What?" she asked, confused.

"I found stab wounds on Dakota when I buried him. It was the same knife, and it had his blood on it. I thought it was Vincent, so I panicked. I left Tommy home with May, and I drove straight to Dr. Freeman's office." His voice choked up. "I found—I found him hung up on a stake in the middle of his office."

"So Vincent is back," Karen said, backing away from him. "He stabbed May."

"No," he said, fighting to get the words out. "It wasn't him. None of it was."

"Then who was it?" Karen said, still backing away from Scott.

He bit his tongue. He knew he had to tell her, but how could he? How could he tell Karen that their son had done this to May, to his own sister? How could Scott tell her that Tommy was sick, just like he once was?

"Who?" Karen pleaded.

Scott winced but forced himself to say it. "Tommy. It was Tommy."

"What?" she said. "No, not Tommy. He wouldn't, you're—you're lying."

"I'm not." He choked on the words as he spoke them. "I came home and found him holding the knife and May bleeding."

"No, no," she said as she hit him on the shoulder. "It's not true, it's not. You're lying."

Scott held her arms as she struggled. He didn't blame her. She needed him to be lying. She needed it not to be true, just as much as he wished that it wasn't.

Finally, she stopped fighting, and he let her go. "Why?" she begged. "Why would he do that?"

"I don't think it was him."

"But you just said—" The words hung in her mouth. "No, that's not possible."

"We both know it is," Scott said quietly. "Tommy has another personality, just like I did. He didn't try to kill May, but whatever else is in his head did."

"But," Karen said, trying to piece it together, "DID isn't hereditary. You got it because of what happened when you were a child. Tommy couldn't inherit that."

"April did," he said plainly. "Think about it. Her intelligence, the way she cares about things—are you saying she doesn't remind you of him sometimes?"

"Okay, yes, she did inherit things from Vincent, but what you're saying—"

"Is no different." Scott took her face in his hands. "She inherited Vincent's intellect, but what if Tommy inherited something else? Something darker. When I came home, I saw Tommy holding the knife, but he didn't know what he had done. He thought he had blacked out and was just having a nightmare."

"That doesn't explain everything else," Karen said, trying to find something, anything, to make it not true. Scott knew what she was trying to do—he had done the same thing himself—but the evidence was overwhelming.

"Think about it. Tommy knew the knife was in the drawer."

"What about the note in the bathroom?"

"When we were in May's room, who wasn't there? April was, we both were, but not Tommy. He's the only one who could have put that note there, while we were in May's room after her nightmare."

The memory came flooding back to him. "Her nightmare," he whispered to himself.

"What is it?" Karen asked, seeing the concern in his face.

He didn't hear her. His mind was racing with thoughts of that night. How May had had a nightmare of him, covered in scars. How she had said he tried to drown her in a pool of blood.

"Oh no," Scott said as he rushed out of the room, followed by Karen. He tore through the hallway, passing April in the waiting room. He ran down the hall, almost tripping over himself as he approached the operating room.

Inside sat May, lying asleep with her eyes closed, next to the machine pumping blood out from her lungs. The machine that was turned off.

Scott grabbed the doorknob, but it was locked. He slammed his body against the door, but it wouldn't open. April had joined them now, and she watched in horror.

The last bit of blood drained from the machine as it stopped pumping entirely. Scott looked through the glass as

May's mouth began to fill up with blood. He slammed on the glass, but it made no difference.

The blood was pouring from May's mouth now. Scott watched, horrified, as her heartbeat monitor began to spike. He slammed on the glass again, but it still didn't budge. Karen stood behind him, frozen in place as she watched her daughter dying.

Scott watched in horror. She never woke up, or made a sound, but her body began shaking violently, gasping for air. Blood spilled out from her mouth, covering her and the floor. Her body distorted in the bed, crying out for even the slightest amount of air. But every breath she took sent more blood down her throat, drowning the life out of her.

Scott picked up a chair from the hallway and slammed it against the window, making a small crack. He slammed it again as May's heartbeat monitor beeped faster. He swung again and again until finally the window cracked, but it didn't break.

Before he could hit it again, he saw that it was too late. May's body went limp on the bed, her eyes rolling back in her head and blood spilling out onto the floor. The pulse on the heart monitor beside her went away as she flatlined, drowned in her own blood.

Scott saw his reflection through the mirror. The cracked glass distorted the reflection, but Scott could still see the face staring back at him. The face that had haunted May's nightmares. The face that was covered in horrific scars. May was right.

He did look like a monster.

Chapter Twelve

Dr. Freeman waited in the therapy office for Scott's parents to arrive. It had been several months since his first session with Scott, and they had made some progress in the sessions since then. The boy was still having nightmares, but they weren't quite as frequent as they had been, only happening a couple of times a week now. He had also begun eating again and was gaining some of his weight back. His ribs now barely showed underneath his skin.

But today wasn't about Scott. Despite the parents' objections, Dr. Freeman had convinced them to bring him up on a different day than normal. One where it wouldn't be Scott at all.

Dr. Freeman hadn't met the other personality since the first visit, and even then it had only been for a moment, but whenever they brought Scott up for therapy, the parents saw fit to tell him everything the other personality did. Evidently, they hadn't yet let go of the fact that he had killed a man in self-defense, torture notwithstanding. But Dr. Freeman had the sneaking suspicion that it was more him not being their son that they took exception to.

But either way, it didn't matter. They were almost here, and Dr. Freeman began setting out the donuts. Scott still hadn't touched them, having already eaten before the previous sessions, but Dr. Freeman set them out all the same.

Dr. Freeman heard a knock at the door, and the parents walked in, with the boy waiting behind them in the hall.

"Hello," Dr. Freeman said.

"I thought these might interest you," the mother said as she shoved papers into his hands.

Dr. Freeman took a moment to look at the pictures drawn in crayon.

"We thought maybe they would change your mind about getting rid of that thing," the father snapped.

Dr. Freeman forced a smile. "Thank you, I will take these into consideration. Now if you'll excuse me, I have a patient waiting out in the hall."

Dr. Freeman pulled out his notepad as the boy sat on the couch.

"Hello, young man, my name is Dr. Freeman. I believe we met a few months ago, if only briefly."

The boy said nothing, instead staring blankly at the floor.

"Might I ask what your name is?" Dr. Freeman said, trying to get a reaction out of him. "Because despite what your father claims, I doubt it's 'Thing.' Unless of course you know a cat who wears a striped top hat, in which case I guess that would make Scott 'Thing 2.'" Dr. Freeman couldn't help but chuckle as he said it, but the boy's expression didn't change. He remained still, looking at the floor.

"Okay, I guess you're not familiar with Dr. Seuss. We'll have to remedy that at some point, but for now, let's just talk. Do you know why you're here?" The boy said nothing. "Okay, I'll go first. I am a therapist. My job is to help sick people get better. For example, I am trying to help Scott get over his bad dreams and fear of crows."

Dr. Freeman examined the boy as he spoke, noticing cuts on his fingertips, and his right hand was twitching, scraping the armrest.

"Is there some area where I could help you, something you are afraid of? Bad dreams, perhaps?"

Dr. Freeman choked on his coffee as the boy looked up from the floor. He didn't look directly at him, instead looking past him at the wall. Even so, the boy's expression caused Dr. Freeman to gasp. It was eerily calm, but there was something else there too. Something darker. He would just have to find it.

The boy looked back down at the floor as Dr. Freeman caught his breath. "I'll take that as a yes. But we'll table that discussion for the moment. Why don't we talk about this?" He held up the picture drawn in crayon, and the boy glanced up at it.

The picture was of the therapy office, and of Dr. Freeman lying dead in the middle of it.

"I have to say, I am in shock," he mused as he pointed to the picture. "I mean, just look at the detail."

The boy wrinkled his brow in confusion. He hadn't been expecting that.

"By my calculations, in our last encounter, you were in this room for all of fifteen seconds, and yet look at this. Perfect." Dr. Freeman spun around in his chair to examine the details

of the room next to the picture. He laughed as he pointed to a small crack in the corner of the ceiling. He turned back around to the boy. "I've been in this office for ten years, and I've never noticed that crack before. And yet," he said, pointing at the crack on the picture, "there it is. Pretty impressive for a fleeting glance."

The boy was still confused by the response but remained silent.

"I only have one tiny problem with this drawing." Dr. Freeman pointed to the drawing of himself. He was lying in a pool of his own blood, with cuts over his entire body, along with some sort of screwdriver. "You see this here?" he said, waiting for the boy to glance at it. "This concerns me. You see"—he smiled at the boy—"you used a gray crayon for my hair. I don't know if I appreciate that." He took off his hat. "I am a little too young to be graying."

The boy still didn't speak, but Dr. Freeman could tell he was more at ease than before. The boy's right hand still twitched as he scraped it across the armrest, but not as much as before.

Dr. Freeman held up the picture to look at it one last time. "Aside from the hair, I'd say it's pretty much perfect. Might as well have been drawn by Vincent Van Gogh himself."

The boy looked up at him. "Vincent."

Dr. Freeman was surprised by the boy's tone of voice. It sounded like he was whispering, despite talking at normal volume. The boy also emphasized certain syllables, making it sound quieter than it actually was.

"You like that name?" he questioned.

The boy nodded.

"Well, then, it's nice to meet you, Vincent."

Vincent nodded as Dr. Freeman smirked.

"Well, now that we have introductions out of the way, what do you say we get into the actual therapy part?"

Vincent nodded. He still didn't look directly at Dr. Freeman, but he did look up more, no longer staring exclusively at the floor and wall.

"So, let's start with an easy one. What is the first thing you remember?"

"A field," Vincent said, still in his whisper tone, pausing for a split second between words. It almost wasn't noticeable. Almost. "There was a scarecrow. A man was there. He hurt me."

"That sounds terrifying. What did you do?" He was still hoping for some sort of physical reaction from Vincent, something to help analyze him, but he stayed motionless.

"Hurt him back."

"How did that make you feel?"

Vincent subtly shrugged on the couch.

"You had to feel something. Was it anger, relief, pleasure, something else?"

"Can I have those?" Vincent asked as he looked at the plate of donuts sitting on the table between them.

"Certainly," Dr. Freeman said, surprised. He knew it was Vincent's clever way to dodge the question, but it didn't matter. He was speaking to him now, and that was progress.

Vincent reached over and grabbed the donut closest to him and bit into it. Dr. Freeman was about to ask him another question when he noticed he was eating fast. "You like donuts, don't you?"

Vincent didn't respond, instead picking up another from the table.

"Back to the question at hand, why did you feel the need to kill the man in that way?"

Vincent stopped eating for a moment and looked straight at him. "He deserved it."

"That may be true, but I suspect it was something else too," Dr. Freeman pushed. "Were there any other reasons you hurt that man?"

Vincent paused. Dr. Freeman could see the look of shame on his face as he looked down at the floor, and he didn't have to say it. Dr. Freeman knew why he had done that to the man. He had wanted to kill him, had needed to.

Dr. Freeman had never expected an answer. All he needed was the reaction, so he moved on to other questions. "How are things going at home? Scott says you two have been talking back and forth with Post-it notes. Is that right?"

"Yes," Vincent said as he grabbed his fourth donut. A small sliver of jelly fell onto his shirt, but he didn't stop to look at it, instead wiping it off with his hand and licking it after he finished the donut.

My word, Dr. Freeman thought. Either the boy had never learned how to eat properly, or he was starving. Dr. Freeman suspected it was both.

"Does Scott give you any messages of particular interest?"

"Like what?"

The voice sent a small chill down Dr. Freeman's spine. He knew it was only a child, but the voice was calm, calculating, almost unnaturally so. It also didn't help that it came from

Scott's body, the scared little kid he had been helping, and yet sounded as distant from Scott's voice as possible.

"I don't know, just anything that you found interesting, I guess."

Vincent shrugged once again. Scott had told Dr. Freeman that they had been exchanging messages, and he was just curious what Vincent would say about the matter. But clearly the boy didn't want to talk about it.

Dr. Freeman watched Vincent carefully as he ate the last donut. Despite holding it with both hands, his right hand still twitched, like he was anxious about something. Dr. Freeman knew what it probably was but didn't want to get into that right now. Instead, he tried to lighten the mood.

"Would you like something to drink?" he asked. "I don't have any water, but I can offer you a cup of coffee." Dr. Freeman wasn't sure about giving an eight-year-old coffee, but he suspected he hadn't been given much to drink today, and it wasn't like he was bursting with energy to begin with.

Vincent nodded, so Dr. Freeman walked over to the coffee machine to pour him a cup. He poured a good amount of creamer in it, as he didn't figure the boy would appreciate black coffee until he was older.

He walked back over to Vincent and handed him the cup. Before he could stop him, Vincent put it to his mouth and poured the scalding hot coffee down his throat.

"No!" Dr. Freeman screamed, but it was too late. Vincent winced in pain as the coffee burned his throat and mouth. He dropped the cup to the floor as Dr. Freeman tried to help. But Dr. Freeman didn't know what to do. He expected Vincent to

scream, but he didn't. Vincent held in the cries as his entire body shook from the pain. Dr. Freeman heard a slight whine coming from him as Vincent reached down and picked the cup back up.

Amazingly, the cup remained unbroken. The coffee, however, had spilled out onto the floor. "Sorry," Vincent said as he winced from the pain of speaking.

Dr. Freeman was amazed. With the degree of the burn in his throat, he hadn't expected him to be able to speak for days. "That's quite alright," he said as he sat back down in his chair. There wasn't much coffee left that Vincent hadn't drunk, and he would just mop it up later, as opposed to taking time out of their session.

"So," Dr. Freeman asked, "Scott tells me you've been having nightmares. Evidently he can see bits and pieces of what you dream about, and I assume it works vice versa. Apparently your nightmares are worse than his."

"Scott is afraid of crows. They keep him up at night."

"Is that why you've been killing them?" Dr. Freeman asked, watching Vincent's reaction. Vincent looked straight up, surprised, but then his expression changed back to normal, without speaking a word. "Your parents told me that they found crows dead in the backyard right after Scott came home from isolation. I assume that was you."

"Yes."

"Why?" Dr. Freeman asked. "If you're not afraid of them, then why did you feel the need to kill them, evidently with rocks?"

Vincent remained silent, looking straight into Dr. Freeman's eyes. He couldn't help but be taken aback. Despite the fact

that it was a boy, the look in his eyes was unlike anything Dr. Freeman had ever seen.

But Vincent had seen him look scared, if for only a moment. Vincent moved his gaze back down to the floor. *Stupid*, Dr. Freeman scolded himself silently. *The boy is already being treated like a monster. The last thing he needs is for his therapist to treat him like one too.* But he couldn't help it. Shivers shot down his spine every time Vincent looked at him. It was like a reflex.

Dr. Freeman forced himself not to quiver as he repeated the question. "Why did you kill the crows, Vincent? Was it because they were scaring Scott?"

Vincent remained silent, staring at the floor.

"Okay, why don't I tell you my theory, then? I think that you killed the crows for two reasons. First, the crows were causing Scott not to sleep, which meant you couldn't come out. I don't think you liked that. But I also think you did it for Scott. Sure, you may have had your own reasons, but if he can feel your dreams, you can feel his. I think you knew how much he was afraid and were trying to help him."

Vincent said nothing.

"Or it could be the third option. You wanted to hurt something, and Scott being afraid of it gave you the excuse." Dr. Freeman looked for a reaction, but Vincent gave him none. "Okay, you don't have to tell me. Just so long as you're not lying to yourself about which one it is."

Vincent looked up. Dr. Freeman tried to force himself not to shudder, but he couldn't help it. Vincent watched as Dr. Freeman's hands shook.

Vincent was looking directly at him, knowing how he would react. That was good, he thought. It meant he had struck a nerve, and Vincent was trying to change the subject. "Let's talk about your nightmares. Scott has told me some of it, but I thought I should hear it from you."

Vincent hesitated to speak, but he could tell Dr. Freeman wasn't going to let it go. "In my dreams..." He paused. "I see blood. It's everywhere. It flows down the walls, drops from the ceiling, pours from the sky." He stopped for a moment and let out a soft sigh. "Drains from the bodies."

Dr. Freeman could feel himself becoming anxious, not because of the dreams themselves but how Vincent sounded describing them, almost as if he enjoyed it. "Whose bodies are they?"

Vincent looked up straight at him. "Everyone."

"That sounds terrifying," Dr. Freeman said, swallowing the lump in his throat. Vincent continued to look straight at him, and Dr. Freeman could see Vincent playing the dreams over in his head. "But they aren't, are they?"

Vincent shook his head no.

"That's why you called them dreams, not nightmares. Because you aren't scared of them." Dr. Freeman paused. "You like them, don't you, Vincent?"

"Yes," he whispered as the look in his eyes became a glare.

It was all Dr. Freeman could do not to drop his pen as he struggled to write down the notes.

After a few moments of silence, Dr. Freeman caught his breath. "Well, I think that's enough for today," he said, standing up. "I will see you again next week." He opened the door for Vincent. As Vincent walked out, Dr. Freeman once

again noticed the scratches on his fingertips, and a horrible thought entered his mind. "Have you killed any crows since I had the first session with Scott?"

"No."

"Why not?"

Vincent said nothing, instead walking down the hall.

Later that day, Dr. Freeman was about to go home when he saw the drawing lying on his desk. He looked at it for a moment, still amazed by the detail. Vincent had even colored the paper underneath the blood black, so the red would appear darker and more crimson.

As Dr. Freeman was about to set it down and leave for the day, he noticed something on it. He looked up to the bookshelf in the corner of the room, gulping nervously. He had been impressed by the detail from the start, but this was different.

The books in the drawing were in perfect order. The color, the size, the ones that were leaning on their edge, acting as bookends. All perfectly drawn. The drawing dropped out of his hand as he looked at them. He had at least a hundred books, sprawled out on the shelf, and in fifteen seconds, Vincent had remembered every single shape, every single color, every single detail in perfect order. That wasn't just intelligence or a good memory. This was something else. Something unnatural.

Something inhuman.

Chapter Thirteen

Scott stood in the morgue. Karen was waiting outside, holding Joey. She couldn't bear to see this. April had wanted to come in to say goodbye to her sister, but he hadn't let her. He wasn't sure how May would look and didn't want to chance April seeing it if it was bad.

The doctor had said it was an equipment malfunction, that the machine pumping the blood out of her lungs had simply stopped working. That didn't feel right to Scott, but what other explanation was there? Tommy was still at the house and couldn't have snuck his way into the operating room even if he had been there. The hospital staff had barely let them into the operating room.

The morgue was dark, its walls gray. It was cold, so much so that he could see his breath. In the corner of the room stood a sink, and opposite that was a blank chalkboard.

The coroner was unlocking the storage drawer the body was being kept in. The doctors had already done their examination and filed her away, but Scott wanted to see her. He had to see her for himself.

The coroner opened the drawer and slid the body out before leaving him alone with her.

A white sheet was covering her body. He lifted up the edge and pulled it down from her face. He turned away at the sight of it, his daughter's face, cold and lifeless, still covered in blood.

Scott closed his eyes as tears fell down his face. How could they show her to him like that? Why wouldn't they clean her first?

Swallowing the lump in his throat, he walked over to the sink and grabbed the hand towel beside it. He poured water on it before walking back over to May's body.

He brushed the blood off her face, forcing himself to look.

The blood was stained on, and it took him almost half an hour to wipe it all off. The hair took the longest. The blood was caked on, but it finally returned to the bright blonde Scott recognized.

He stood over her body as he dropped the towel to the floor. He wanted to say something, to tell her he loved her one last time, but he couldn't.

Scott leaned down over her and kissed her on the forehead. "My brave girl," he said, his voice cracking, before sliding the white sheet back over her.

As he walked out of the morgue, he noticed the chalkboard in the corner. It was no longer blank. He looked in horror at the words scribbled on it. *Like Father.*

Outside, Karen and April waited for him in the hallway. They said nothing as they embraced, crying on each other's shoulders.

Morning was close, but the moon still dominated the sky. Moonlight poured down through the clouds as the car pulled up in their driveway. The outside air was cold, and the wind blew leaves across the street.

No one had said anything on the ride back. What was there to say? Scott put the car in park, hesitating to get out. He turned around to face April in the back seat. "There's something you should know."

Karen turned to look at Scott, nodding that it was time.

"What is it?" April asked.

Scott told her everything. She deserved to know. He should have told her a long time ago, he thought. Maybe things would have been different.

She sat quietly for a moment, taking it all in. She had known Scott had been taken when he was young, but not about Vincent.

They had always planned on telling her. They were just waiting for her to be old enough. But then, after "it" had happened, they'd decided it was better to bury it in the past.

"So, you think Tommy inherited DID from you?" she asked.

"Yes," Scott said. He could see her mind going through possible scenarios.

"So, it wasn't Tommy who"—she hesitated, forcing the words—"hurt May, it was this other personality. The one like Vincent."

He nodded.

"So, Tommy just has to get rid of the other identity, the darker one," she stated. "Right?"

"It's not that simple," Scott said. "One personality can't just 'get rid' of the other. It doesn't work like that."

"Okay, but you said you and Dr. Freeman killed Vincent. We just have to do whatever you and he did to Tommy."

Scott didn't like the word she used. Kill. It sounded more violent than it needed to, but she was right. A feeling of guilt rushed over him. He had killed Vincent. He had never thought of it that way before. No, he thought, he couldn't think like that. He hadn't killed him. He'd just told Dr. Freeman what Vincent had done.

"We can't just do what Dr. Freeman did," he told April. "It's more complicated."

"But you said it was a mental procedure, not a surgical one."

"Yes, but even if we had the medicine to put him out, it wouldn't work without Dr. Freeman there. We couldn't do whatever psychological things Dr. Freeman had to do. It won't work without a therapist."

"How do you know?" April asked.

The memory came flooding back to Scott, but he pushed it out of his mind. "I just do, okay? We can't do it without Dr. Freeman. That's probably why Tommy—the other personality—killed him. We can't do anything right now."

"Okay," April said.

Scott could see her mind still racing. If there was a way, she would find it. She got that from Vincent too.

They walked up to the doorstep. Karen's hands were shaking as she grabbed the doorknob. "Whatever we see in there, whatever he does, he is still our son," she said before looking at April, "and he is still your brother. He is sick, but it's not his fault." Scott knew she was reassuring herself more than she was them.

Karen opened the door, and they walked in. April turned on the lights, which flickered dimly, lighting up the spinning blades of the ceiling fan, which creaked as they turned.

The light also revealed the rope that had been tied to the fan, as well as Tommy's corpse that hung from it.

April screamed as she saw it. The neck seemingly stretched out from the body, wrung tightly by the thick rope. Tommy's limbs hung down limp from his corpse as it slowly spun around. His face was pale and his eyes glazed over, almost as if he was still watching them.

Scott walked over to him and cut him down. He laid Tommy's body on the floor and shut his eyes.

Why would he have done this? Why would the other personality kill himself? Unless, Scott thought as a horrifying realization set in, it wasn't the other personality. Tommy must've realized what he had done and couldn't take it.

No, no, why did you leave him here alone? Scott scolded himself. *Why didn't you help him?*

Scott was still standing over Tommy's body when he heard the gun cock behind him. He turned around to see Karen standing in front of the door, pointing the shotgun at him, and April holding Joey behind her.

"What are you doing?" Scott asked in disbelief.

"You did this," Karen said. "You killed him."

"What? No," he said, his face wrinkling with confusion. "He must've realized what the other personality had done and hung himself."

"Look around the room, Scott," she said, her voice quivering.

He looked around, seeing the same pictures on the floor as when he'd left with April, along with the moved furniture and the broken glass table.

"There was a struggle." She was almost crying as she said it. "That doesn't happen if you commit suicide."

Scott shook his head no.

"That happens when someone kills you."

"You think I did this?" he asked. "How?"

"I think someone did," she said, her voice still cracking. The shotgun shook in her hands as she held it towards him. "I think you did this before you brought May to the hospital. I think you've been changing."

"That's not possible," Scott said. "You know I haven't been sleeping, and I haven't blacked out."

April stood nervously behind Karen, holding Joey in her arms. "Mom?" she asked.

"How can you be sure? I mean, really sure? You've been hallucinating. How do you know you haven't switched during one of them?"

"Because..." Scott hesitated. "Because I know Vincent. I know his thoughts. If he came out, even for a second, I would know, because I would feel him crawling his way out. He has forced a switch before, you know that." He stepped closer to her as tears fell down her face. "And trust me, that's not a feeling I will ever forget."

Karen tried to hold the gun steady, but her hands were shaking. "How do I know you aren't him right now?"

Scott stepped closer to her, the barrel pressing against his chest. "Because you know me, and you know him. You've always known."

He paused as he grabbed the gun barrel and slowly lowered it. "Truth be told, I think deep down, you knew before he even told you."

Karen didn't fight him as he moved the barrel down. He knew she wouldn't. She had always been able to tell, but deep down, he knew that it wouldn't have mattered either way. She couldn't have shot either one of them.

She dropped the shotgun and hugged him.

April had walked over to Tommy's corpse and knelt down beside him.

She started crying, making Joey cry in her arms. Karen took Joey from her as Scott walked up to her.

"I teased him," she said as she burst into tears. "Why did I do that? I should—"

"Shh," Scott said as he placed his hand on her shoulder. "Don't say that. You were his sister, and he loved you. Nothing could change that."

They stood silently for a moment, mourning, until something crashed into the door.

They turned to face the door in an instant, moonlight seeping through the glass at the top of the door.

Something hit it again.

Scott leaned down to pick up the shotgun as Karen motioned to go up the stairs. They walked up the steps backwards, the shotgun trained on the door.

The sound of the door crashing open echoed through the house, and as it slammed against the wall, Scott saw the shadow of something walking in.

Karen, still holding Joey, ran to the main bedroom with April, followed by Scott. He locked the door behind him. They

crouched in the opposite corner, by the window, and Scott kept his gun trained on the door.

They could hear the stairs creaking as something walked up them. Moonlight was pouring in through the window beside them, lighting up the floor in front of the door. Scott could hear himself breathing as the creaking stopped. It was in the hallway.

Everything was silent for a moment, and then suddenly the door shook. It sounded as if a jackhammer was tearing into it. Scott took a deep breath, waiting for the door to crash open.

Then something hit the window. A crow crashed into it, causing the hairline crack the crow had previously left in it to expand. It crashed into it again, almost in rhythm with the door.

Crash.

Karen was beside Scott, trying to keep Joey quiet as he tried to burst into tears. April was crouching behind him as he sat still, waiting for it to happen.

Crash.

No one could breathe as they waited in terror.

Crash. The door flew open, and something stood in the doorway.

Scott could see the outline of a man in the darkness, but the moonlight didn't reach him yet.

The crow crashed through the window, screeching as it flew across the room and landed on the man's shoulders.

Scott sat paralyzed for a moment as the man stepped closer. He couldn't see his face yet, but he could see a long black coat stretching down to the floor, with crows' feathers sticking out from it like a pelt.

Scott forced himself out of his fear-induced paralysis and tightened his grip on the shotgun. He pointed the barrel up at the man's chest and squeezed the trigger.

Misfire.

The shotgun burned in Scott's hands and dropped to the floor. There was no time to pick it back up and try again.

The man stepped closer, inching toward the light as he whispered calmly, "Hello, Scott."

He recognized the voice. The voice he had heard in his head over the years. *No*, he thought, *it can't be.*

The man stepped into the moonlight, revealing his face. It was littered with scars, and the life had seemed to drain out of it, but it looked all too familiar.

Scott wiped his eyes with his hand before looking back up. It wasn't real, he told himself. He was seeing things. But the man still stood there. No, that wasn't possible, it couldn't be real, Scott thought—until he saw Karen.

Karen held her mouth with her hand as she looked at the man, then back at Scott. She couldn't breathe as she looked back and forth in disbelief. She looked at Scott once more before turning her head back across the room, facing the man, her voice more confused than scared.

"Vincent?"

Chapter Fourteen

"Vincent?" Karen asked in disbelief as she looked at him standing in the moonlight, like a wild animal searching for its next victim.

His face was littered with gruesome scars that distorted his features, twisting them into something almost unrecognizable. His skin was pale, and his black hair appeared coarse in the moonlight, but there was no mistaking it. It was him. The moonlight cast a shadow over the crow standing on his shoulder, making its monstrous wings appear stretched out over the entire room.

Scott looked in horror at Vincent standing across the room, wearing his face and yet looking completely different. He wanted to speak, but his body was frozen in complete shock.

"Hello, Karen," Vincent said as he looked across the room but stopped short of looking directly at her.

The moonlight glowed off her silky black hair as she looked at Vincent. Feathers fell from his black coat onto the white carpet beneath them. Shattered glass from the window was scattered across the floor, and wind gushed in, blowing Karen's hair as she stood beside it.

Scott looked at Vincent, telling himself he wasn't there, that this was just a hallucination. But he knew the truth. Karen saw him too. Karen saw both of them. "No," Scott said. "You can't be here."

Vincent said nothing as he stepped toward Scott, his head tilted sideways to examine him.

They looked at each other for a moment, each taking it in. It was strange to see each other like this, face-to-face, while at the same time, it was unsettling. It was like looking in a mirror, except this time, the mirror looked back.

Scott could hear April breathing behind him, but she didn't dare say anything, afraid of the consequences. Joey started crying in her arms, and she rocked him slowly, trying to quiet him.

His cries echoed throughout the house as Vincent stepped closer. The cold, piercing wind blew across him, rustling the crow's feathers. As Vincent stepped past Scott and closer to April, Scott and Karen remained frozen in shock. They looked at each other, not knowing what to say.

Vincent stopped in front of April, who looked up at him with fear in her eyes. The crow on his shoulder twisted its head backwards, keeping its gaze on Scott.

Vincent said nothing as he reached his hand over to her cheek. She tried to move back, but she was against the wall. There was nowhere to go. His hand grazed her cheek softly as he looked at her, his expression calm yet horrifying.

Scott watched from behind him, his heart pounding in his chest, waiting to see what Vincent was going to do. He could feel his lungs fighting for air, but he wasn't able to breathe.

Vincent closed his eyes for a moment and sighed, standing in front of April, before opening them again. Vincent took his hand from her cheek and looked down at the baby in her arms, a boy only a few months old. He turned back toward Scott. "Cute kid."

Scott swallowed the lump in his throat. "How—how are you here?"

Vincent stepped closer to him. "All in good time. But trust me..." He leaned over, his face mere inches from Scott's. "That's the least of your worries."

Karen walked over to Vincent, stopping in front of him as he turned to face her. She touched her hand to his face, seeing if he was real. Her voice cracked as she spoke. "Did you kill them?" she asked. "Did you kill our children?"

Vincent looked down below her, not looking her in the eyes. "Yes."

Tears streamed down Karen's face. "Why? Why are you doing this?"

Vincent didn't answer her. He turned to face Scott and outstretched his hand, taking him by the throat and walking him across the room, backing him up against the wall. Scott's spine pressed up against it, cracking painfully. Karen reached for the shotgun, but the crow flew down, resting on top of it.

She backed away from it, her arms stretched out, almost trying to shield April in case something happened. Joey had stopped crying. The only sound left in the room was Scott struggling to breathe with Vincent's hand on his throat.

"You can't be here," he grunted. "It's not possible."

Vincent tightened his grip on Scott's throat. "Everything's possible, Scott. You just have to look hard enough."

Scott struggled to get free, but Vincent's grip wrapped around his throat like a python, suffocating him. He couldn't breathe, much less fight back.

"Let him go," Karen said as she pulled a pistol out of the bedside drawer. It was a silver revolver with a black handle. In its chamber were four rounds, leaving one chamber empty to act as a safety. She raised it toward Vincent, aiming it at his chest.

Scott watched her, knowing that she could never do it. Despite everything, she couldn't see the monster that he was. She had never been able to see it.

She tightened her grip on the trigger, the hammer pulling back halfway. Vincent watched, waiting for it. She closed her eyes and tried to force herself to pull the trigger, but she couldn't.

She dropped the gun to the floor, the silver revolver bouncing off the carpet. Vincent turned back toward Scott, looking at the expression on his face. Scott had known Karen couldn't shoot Vincent, and now they both did.

Scott could feel his heart pounding as he waited to see what Vincent was going to do. Vincent's mouth shook as he found the words, looking straight into Scott's eyes.

"Did you even hesitate?" he whispered. "Did you even hesitate to kill me?"

Scott fought against Vincent's grip on his neck, trying to speak. "You skinned those people alive."

"They deserved it."

"You would have done the same to them," Scott said, motioning toward Karen and April. "It was just a matter of time."

"No." There was pain in Vincent's voice, despite him remaining calm. "That's not true. That's what you told yourself. Your excuse to get rid of me."

"You would have," Scott said. "You may not have wanted to, but sooner or later you would have. You can't slip back as far as you did and still come back."

"Why?" Vincent growled. "Because Dr. Freeman said so? Because the trash that kidnapped us couldn't?"

"Because I know you," Scott said, choking. "No matter how much you tried to fight it, your dreams always came back, even before it happened."

"So?" Vincent said as his hand started to twitch.

Scott didn't know what to say. He knew that Vincent couldn't see what he was becoming. If he hadn't stopped it, Vincent would've lost control.

"Why did you make Tommy like you?" Scott asked. "Why did you make him kill May?"

"Like me?" Vincent said, feigning confusion. "Killing his family? He gets that from you, Scott."

The wind was blowing harder now, shaking the furniture. The sound of it rumbling echoed through the house as Vincent let go of his grip. Scott dropped to the floor, gasping for breath. Air felt like sandpaper going into his lungs, and his throat still ached, as if a noose was coiled around it.

"How?" Scott asked. "How did you make him do that?"

Vincent walked closer to Karen as April crouched down by the wall, still holding Joey. Scott stood, trying to protect them, but fell back to the floor as the crow flew in front of him.

"Like I said," Vincent said as he walked up to Karen, putting a knife to her throat, "all in good time."

"No, please," Scott begged. "Don't hurt her."

Vincent pulled Karen in front of him, pressing the knife against her throat. "Come stop me," he said, watching Scott on the other side of the room. Scott stood up to walk, but the crow spread its wings in front of him and screeched. His fear kept him from moving.

Blood had dripped from the small cut on Karen's neck as Vincent watched Scott stop in fear of the crow. Vincent pressed the knife tighter to her neck. He knew the crow would keep Scott from doing anything, but that wasn't the point.

Scott recognized the knife. The same kitchen knife, still stained with May's blood. He wanted to do something, anything, to help her, but he couldn't. He was ashamed, but no matter how hard he fought, the fear of the crow paralyzed his body in place.

"Please," Scott begged. "She had nothing to do with it, I swear. It was my decision, not hers."

There it was.

"Hurt me," Scott pleaded. "Please, hurt me."

Vincent lowered the knife and released his grip on Karen, dropping her to the floor. She knelt down, feeling the blood from her neck, as Vincent stepped toward Scott.

"Oh, I am going to hurt you, Scott." Vincent stepped closer to him, backing him back up against the wall. The room grew darker as the moonlight disappeared, covered by clouds that poured down rain. The wind blew the rain inside, soaking the bedroom and causing the smell of damp wood.

Scott's back hit the wall as the crow began scraping its talons across the floor.

Sccrrreeee

"But you see," Vincent said as he put his arm across Scott's throat and leaned down, looking at the scared reflection of himself, "I'm not going to torture you. I'm not even going to kill you." Vincent pushed his arm further on Scott's throat, cutting off his oxygen, causing his head to burn in fiery pain. "I'm going to do to you what you did to me."

Sccrrreeee

Vincent was inches from Scott's face as he spoke. "I am going to rip away everything you care about, piece by piece, limb by limb. I am going take everyone you ever loved away from you, like you took them from me."

Sccrrreeee

Vincent whispered into Scott's ear, his pace increasing. "I will take Karen, and April, and the baby, until you are left alone, having watched them die, knowing it was because of you. I will turn your life into a living nightmare that you won't be able to wake up from, and then, when you are left alone, when your entire world has been clawed away, and the blood stains your hands, then you will understand what it's like to feel completely alone."

Vincent let go, and Scott fell to the floor, gasping for air. His head was on fire, and his lungs felt like concrete in his chest.

"I have thought of nothing else for seven years," Vincent growled as he leaned down to look at Scott writhing on the floor. "No matter what you do, no matter how hard you try to save them, there is no escape from this."

Vincent turned around and walked across the room. Rain was flooding in now, soaking the room and everyone in it. The crow's black feathers dripped water as it took its place back on his shoulder. Vincent pushed past Karen and grabbed April by the hair, dragging her behind him. April set Joey on the floor as she was dragged sideways. Karen tried to stop him, but he pushed her backwards into the wall.

"Help!" April screamed as Vincent dragged her to the doorway, where she began clawing at the walls, trying to escape his grip. Scott stood up, running toward her, but the crow beat its wings and took flight, slamming into Scott, knocking him back onto the floor and staying on him until Vincent dragged April into the hallway, her screams echoing off the walls. The door slammed itself behind them.

Scott screamed as the crow attacked him. It tore into his skin with its talons before taking flight out the window. He jumped up and ran for the door, but Vincent was gone, and April with him.

Scott stood at the doorway, looking out into an empty hallway, as Karen crawled across the floor behind him to pick up Joey. She cradled him in her arms as she looked into the hallway, another one of her children gone. She fought back the tears as she looked down at Joey, who was crying in her arms.

"Don't cry."

Chapter Fifteen

It had been many years since Dr. Freeman's first session with Vincent. He had made progress with Scott, getting his dreams to subside almost completely, but Vincent was a different story.

Despite his attempts to help him, he hadn't made any real progress. He tried his best to make him feel as normal as he could, hoping it would help him, but it hadn't. Whatever progress he made had been undone by the lowlifes Scott called parents. Dr. Freeman didn't know exactly what they were doing. Neither Scott nor Vincent would tell him, but he knew it wasn't good. He wasn't sure if Scott knew himself, but he never felt it was his place to ask.

Dr. Freeman had hoped it would get better once college started. Scott had decided to stay on campus, and that meant Vincent would finally get to leave his house and actually attend school. From what Dr. Freeman understood, the parents had explained the situation to the teachers, and Scott had gone to school every other day, keeping Vincent at home, where he couldn't hurt anyone.

Idiots. How could they expect someone to conquer their own demons if they weren't even allowed outside interaction? But despite his pleas against it, they had done it all the same.

But even getting away from them, Vincent hadn't gotten better. His dreams of torturing and killing were just as strong as ever. Or at least they had been, until—

"Good morning, Vincent," Dr. Freeman said as Vincent walked into his office. "How are you doing?"

"Good," Vincent said as he sat down on the couch.

Dr. Freeman walked over to the coffeepot and poured himself a cup before pouring an extra cup for Vincent. He handed Vincent his coffee and sat down in his chair. "How's college going?"

"Fine."

"Just fine?" Dr. Freeman asked. "Scott tells me you have been doing exceptionally well. Which, considering you never went to school before, is quite an achievement."

"Scott exaggerates," Vincent said as he drank his coffee.

"Really?" Dr. Freeman said as he looked over his notes from his last session with Scott. "So you haven't earned a perfect score on every test you've taken so far?"

Vincent shrugged. His hand still twitched, scratching the armrest.

"Okay," Dr. Freeman said, "let's move on to more pressing matters. Have you told her yet?"

Vincent's eyes shot up, straight at him. Even after all these years, he still had to fight not to shudder.

"I'll take that as a no." Dr. Freeman wrote it down on his notepad and looked back up towards Vincent. "May I ask why not?"

Vincent said nothing as he looked down at the floor, seeing how Dr. Freeman looked at him.

"Fine, you don't have to tell me," Dr. Freeman said as he finished his coffee and set his brown hat on the table beside him. His black hair was graying, and his coat was faded. "Let's talk about your dreams. You do still have them, correct?"

"Yes."

"Why do you think that is?"

Vincent chuckled under his breath. "You're the therapist."

Dr. Freeman laughed. "Well, I suppose you're right." He shifted in his chair. "Scott's nightmares are a manifestation of his inner fears, and once I was able to get him to see that, they went away. Not completely, mind you, but to a degree. But yours are different. They aren't nightmares, they are dreams, which makes it more complicated."

"Why?" Vincent asked as he looked down at the floor. "I think about killing people during the day, and I dream about it at night. What part of that is complicated?"

Dr. Freeman looked at him with sympathy, seeing the guilt inside him. "The part where you haven't done it yet."

"What's that supposed to mean?" Vincent asked as his hand started twitching more.

"It can mean lots of things. Maybe you just haven't had the right opportunity. Maybe you're just biding your time. Or maybe the reason you haven't killed anyone is that, deep down, you don't want to."

Vincent said nothing.

Dr. Freeman could tell he wasn't going to prove anything to Vincent this way, so he decided to take another route. "Why don't you tell me about her?"

Dr. Freeman waited for a response, but none came. "You don't have anything to say? Scott was quite talkative about her in our last session. It seems he is quite smitten." He watched for a reaction, anything to help him understand, but Vincent remained motionless. "Scott tells me that 'you' have been out with her several times. You don't have anything to say?"

Vincent's head tilted slightly as he looked at the floor.

"She still doesn't know about you, does she?" He looked at Vincent, trying to get a read. "You should tell her."

"Why?" Vincent said, his voice cold. "So she can look at me the way everyone else does?" He looked Dr. Freeman in the eyes, watching him shudder. "The way you do."

"That's not fair," he said, trying to hide the chill going down his spine at the sound of Vincent's voice.

Vincent's hand started to twitch more as his voice grew colder. "So you don't think I'm a monster?"

"Of course not."

"Really?" Vincent said. "Then why do you have a plan to kill me?"

"What?" Dr. Freeman said, shocked. "I don't have a plan to kill you."

"Don't lie to me," Vincent said slowly.

"I'm not lying."

Vincent's eyes cut from Dr. Freeman to the bookcase behind him. "Top shelf, three over from the right. Green cover. It's a book about split personalities."

"That's just for research purposes. I have to know about the disease if I'm going to help you." Dr. Freeman scolded himself. He shouldn't have said *disease*.

"Okay." Vincent's glare returned to Dr. Freeman. "Then tell me why it only has one crease in the spine. One page that you turned to frequently. From the looks of it, page eighty-three. So tell me, what is on that page?"

Dr. Freeman could feel his heartbeat quicken. Vincent's hand was starting to twitch more violently, his tone growing more lifeless. "Vincent?"

"It wouldn't happen to be the page on how to kill another personality, would it?"

"Vincent," Dr. Freeman repeated, trying to calm him down.

"It wouldn't be the page that says in order to kill me, you would first have to inject me with a special chemical, one that would put me in a state of suggestion, while also not letting me switch to Scott."

"Vincent, don't."

"The same chemical that you purchased a few months after I became your 'patient.' I saw the receipt on your desk. I also know that you keep it in the bottom drawer, because when you open it, I can hear liquid moving. You can lie and say it's just one of your bottles of liquor, but we both know you keep that in your top drawer, for those days when I remind you too much of"—the words choked in his mouth—"him."

"Do you think you are like 'him,' Vincent?"

Vincent's head tilted back and forth as his hand twitched faster. "Maybe."

Dr. Freeman leaned forward in his chair. "Then do it."

Vincent looked at him, shocked. "Do what?"

"What you're thinking of doing right now. Killing me." Dr. Freeman watched as Vincent's twitching got more erratic. "Come on. You think I don't know what it means when your hand is twitching? You think I don't know that there isn't a moment that goes by that you aren't thinking about it? Killing someone? That feeling you would get?"

"Stop."

"We both know you're smart enough to get away with it. I bet you could do it right here and still not get caught."

"Stop," Vincent pleaded.

"How would you do it? You must have thought of hundreds of ways by now. Would you cave in my skull on the corner on the desk? Or would you break that coffee cup on the table and use it to slit my throat?"

"Stop talking," Vincent pleaded as he held his head in pain, trying to resist it.

"No, that would be too quick, wouldn't it? You like to take your time. You'd probably just stab me in my kidneys and watch me bleed out onto the floor for hours." Dr. Freeman took out a pocket knife and set it on the table.

The room got silent as Vincent looked at the knife.

"Come on, there's no sense in waiting. If this is what you want, if this is who you are, then do it."

Vincent reached over and picked up the knife. He barely heard Dr. Freeman anymore, his thoughts consumed by it. Longing for it. But he was hesitating. Something was holding him back.

"Do it!" Dr. Freeman screamed. He could see the look in Vincent's eyes, one of pure darkness.

Vincent's grip tightened on the knife.

"I just hope you can look Karen in the eyes afterwards."

Dr. Freeman smiled as the knife fell out of Vincent's hand, as he fell back into the chair, his hand no longer twitching.

Dr. Freeman chuckled to himself. "That's what I thought. Just in time, too. I thought I might have to buy a new couch."

Vincent was out of breath as everything became clear again. The longing was gone, replaced by something else.

"You see, Vincent, there is a difference between you and my former patient. If I had given him a knife, he would've killed me without hesitation. Whereas you, despite all your demons trying to claw their way out, didn't."

After a few more moments, Dr. Freeman sighed. "I did research a way to get rid of you. And for that I am truly sorry, but I needed to have a way to stop you in case my original impression of you was wrong."

"Which was?" Vincent asked.

"That despite your darker impulses, you care about people. You care about Scott. That's the only reason you've been able to hang on this long. But now I think there is someone else."

Vincent looked to the floor at the mention of her.

Dr. Freeman reached into his briefcase and pulled out a drawing. "Scott gave this to me during his last session. Said he thought I might find it interesting."

Vincent looked up at the picture he had drawn.

"I must say, while your previous drawings were impressive, I very much prefer your new subject matter." Dr. Freeman smiled as he looked at the hand-drawn picture of Karen. "She is quite lovely."

Dr. Freeman got up and handed the picture over to Vincent as their session was coming to a close. "You should tell her. She might surprise you."

Vincent set his coffee cup on the table and shook Dr. Freeman's hand before walking toward the door.

Dr. Freeman was walking to his desk when a thought occurred to him.

"If I may be so bold, how did you know that the procedure was on page eighty-three?"

Vincent didn't answer as the memory came flooding back to him.

Chapter Sixteen

"How is he back?" Karen asked Scott as they paced the bedroom floor. Joey had finally stopped crying, and they had put him in his crib in the next room so he could go to sleep while they figured out what to do. The window was still broken from the crow, and they stepped around the glass scattered across the white carpet.

"I don't know," Scott said. His mind was racing with possible answers, but none of them made sense. "You saw him too, so he isn't in my head."

"Maybe we're both hallucinating from lack of sleep and the stress of losing"—her voice quivered—"losing the kids."

"The same hallucination?" he asked. "Not possible. Besides, he took April; that couldn't have been a hallucination. Maybe it was a lookalike. Maybe someone dressed up like him, trying to scare us or something."

Karen shook her head. "I saw his eyes, Scott. It was him."

"Okay," he said, sitting down on the edge of the bed. A memory was trying to push its way into his head, but he couldn't reach it. Something from the crash, something he'd forgotten.

"We know it was him," she said, sitting on the bed beside Scott. "We know it was Vincent." A tear fell down her face when she thought about it. "How could he do this? After everything, how could he do that to May and Tommy?"

Scott put his arm around her. "It's who he is. Who he's always been."

"I don't believe that."

"I know," he said as he wiped the tears off her face. "But it doesn't change the fact that he murdered the man that kidnapped us, or those men that he skinned alive. It doesn't change the fact that he killed our children."

"Our?" she said under her breath.

Scott didn't hear her. "I don't know how he's back, but we can't let him kill anyone else. We have to get April back, and then we have to figure out a way to get rid of Vincent."

"You mean kill him," Karen said. "Not get rid of, you mean kill him again."

Kill. That caused Scott to hesitate. She had said kill, the same word April had used. Maybe they were right.

"I won't let him hurt you," he said finally. "I promise."

"Scott," she said as she looked back into his eyes. "He was never the one who hurt me."

The words stung like needles in his heart. She was right. What he had done had hurt her. It had hurt everyone, even the kids, despite them not knowing. But there had been no other way. She couldn't see what Vincent was, what he was becoming. Scott never wanted to get rid of Vincent, but after what he had done to those men, there was no coming back. It was just like Dr. Freeman had told him about the other man.

He wanted to say something to Karen, to tell her how sorry he was that he'd had to make the choice, but he couldn't find the words. Nothing he could say would help her understand.

Joey woke up in the next room and started crying. Karen got up and went to him. Scott sat alone on the bed, trying to think. There had to be a reason Vincent was back. But his mind kept drifting to Tommy and May. Their lifeless eyes haunted his thoughts as he tried to think. Was it his fault? Vincent had killed them to make him suffer, because of what Scott had done.

No, it was Vincent. It was just who he was. Getting back at Scott was just another excuse, like when he'd killed the man, and what he had done after—after April was—after it had happened.

Scott's head pounded in his skull as he sat on the edge of the bed. Why now? Why was Vincent back now? How had he made Tommy kill his sister and write those words on the wall? It didn't make any sense.

As he sat there thinking, he felt something warm on his hand. He looked down and saw blood streaming down his forearm once again. It wasn't as much the last time, but it dripped down from his fingers all the same. He stood up and went to wipe it off. He didn't want to drip blood across the floor to the bathroom, and he remembered that Karen sometimes kept a towel in her drawer to wipe off her makeup at night. He thought he would use it to stop the bleeding long enough to get to the bathroom without spilling blood everywhere.

He reached down to her nightstand and opened up the top drawer. As he looked inside, he stepped back, horrified

by what he saw. There was no towel, nothing to wipe off the blood. There was nothing in the drawer at all, save a single book. A book with a bright red cover, black lettering, and a gold wrap around its base.

Scott picked up the book in horror and thumbed through the pages. Weird symbols littered the coarse, almost yellow paper, contrasting with the blotchy black ink. The book was about two inches thick, and heavy. The cover was worn, and the spine was almost stripped away completely due to the age of the book. At a glance, it would appear that the book was centuries old. At more than a glance, it would appear older. He felt his lungs tighten as he read the title.

Devils and Witchcraft: The Resurrection of Souls.

He continued to skim over the pages. The paper was ancient, and the ink was dried out to the point that it was almost unreadable, but he could make out enough. Enough to know this was how Vincent had come back. He continued to flip through pages until he got to it—the section on resurrection. He turned the page and saw the pages had been ripped out.

Scott set the book down on the bed, trying to think, when he looked back at the open drawer of the nightstand. He hadn't realized it until that moment. The book was in Karen's drawer.

Karen walked back into the room after getting Joey back to sleep to find Scott sitting on the bed, blood still trickling down his arm. He said nothing as he stared at the wall in silence.

She rushed over to him, grabbing a towel from the bathroom to wipe the blood off his arm. "Are you okay?" she asked as the towel became stained with red.

He still said nothing as he looked at the wall, his eyes foggy.

"Scott, what's wrong?"

"Two of our children are dead," he said plainly. "Do you realize that?"

She glared at him, dropping the towel to the floor. "Why would you ask me something like that?"

He swallowed and looked over at her, raising the book up with his right hand. "Found your book."

"What are you talking about?" she asked.

"Your book," he said, eerily calm. "The one you used to bring Vincent back." He threw the book at her lap.

She thumbed through the pages, realizing what the book was. "Scott, I've never seen this book before in my life."

"Stop lying to me!" He screamed as he stood up, startling Karen. "I found that in your drawer, with pages ripped out. I know you did it."

"Did what?" she asked, her tone sharp.

"You couldn't accept that he was sick," Scott growled, ignoring her question. "You couldn't see what he was, so you decided to bring him back."

"Scott, I don't know what you are talking about." Her tone was calm, but her expression was one of anger.

"Makes sense," he went on. "You thought maybe if you brought him back, everything would go back to how it was. Except you couldn't see that he was always going to kill us. No matter what he said, how hard he fought it, he would have killed again. And now, because of it, our children are dead."

Karen slapped him, tears running down her face. "How dare you? How dare you say that to me?"

"Are you really going to deny it to my face?" he asked.

She had her hand over her mouth, trying and failing to remain calm. Her voice was shaky. "Scott, I don't know how that book got in my drawer, or what you think I did with it, but I have never seen it before."

"What about everything else?" he asked. "What about how you've been acting this past week?"

"Scott," she said, anger entering her voice. "I would stop talking."

"Why?" He barely realized what he was saying anymore; his adrenaline had gotten too high. "Are you going to tell me that you haven't been acting different this past week?"

Karen said nothing as tears started to fall from her face. How could he say this to her?

"You act cold to me for seven years, and then all of a sudden you act like my wife again. Like how you acted back when he was still around. Did you think I care about you so little that I wouldn't notice?"

"You almost died, Scott. When you crashed, I almost lost you too. So I'm sorry if I acted a little different, but don't blame me for what you did. If you hadn't killed Vincent, none of this would be happening."

"If I hadn't killed Vincent, he would have killed you!" Scott realized he'd said *killed* for the first time, but he didn't stop. "He would have killed you, and April, and Tommy, and May, and everyone else he could find, because that's who he was, whether you saw it or not."

"You don't know that!" she screamed.

"Yes, I do!" He took a second to regroup his thoughts. "I told you, his dreams had come back. He wanted to hurt someone,

he needed to, and after what he did to those men, he couldn't have stopped himself from hurting someone else."

"He wouldn't have hurt me. Or the kids."

"He's doing it right now! Getting back at me is just his excuse to kill, because that's who he is!"

They both stood quietly for a moment, taking in all that had been said. They were both out of breath, not having had time to grieve for their children. They barely knew what they were saying, but it didn't matter. They said it all the same.

Scott took a deep breath before asking one final question. "Did you cut my brakes?"

Karen's eyes widened in genuine surprise. "What?"

"When the car drove off the road, the brakes didn't work. Vincent couldn't have done it, because the book wasn't checked out until the night of the crash. So, did you cut them?"

She stepped back, not knowing what to say. She bit her lip as tears streamed down her face. Her voice cracked as she looked at him. "How could you think that? How could you think that I would—" She started to cry.

He stepped towards her, but she backed away from him.

"Don't touch me," she said through her tears. Scott tried to say something, but she cut him off. "Just go," she pleaded.

Scott grabbed the book from the bed and walked out of the house. The last thing he heard as he stepped out the door was Joey waking up in his room, crying for his mom.

Chapter Seventeen

Scott pulled up to the library. It had taken him a while to find it from the address scribbled on the library stamp on the inside cover, but he finally had. It was out in the middle of nowhere, surrounded only by trees and dirt as well as the gravel road Scott had driven down to get to it.

The building was one story, but wide. It was made of red bricks that were old and cracking, and its roof was a long blanket of shingles, most of them torn up or missing completely. There were no windows; no outside light came in at all. The steps up to it were concrete, and spaced a little too far apart to walk up smoothly.

Scott approached the old cedar door, with rusted hinges and a handle that was tilted too far to the right. He took a deep breath and walked in.

Truth be told, he didn't know what he expected to find. It was just the only place he'd thought of to go after the fight. He sighed. The fight. He regretted saying the things he said. He could still see the hurt in her eyes when he'd accused her of those things. Maybe he should have stayed, tried to apologize.

No, he thought. If the book had brought Vincent back, then this was where he needed to be—in the library, searching for answers.

Scott walked deeper into the library, seeing the checkout desk at the entrance. It was about four feet long and made of coarse oak wood. An old computer sat atop it, turned on. The computer was several models back. They probably couldn't afford a newer one, from the look of the place. Behind the desk sat a single chair, black and rotating, but it was empty. No one was there.

He glanced at the desk for a moment, surprised. Even though it was late, or early, depending on how you looked at it, the library was still open, and it seemed odd that no one sat there to greet him or check out a book. Although, now that he looked around, he noticed that no one was here at all, no staff, no patrons, nothing. And yet the lights were on. Dim, but on.

Scott looked at the book in his hand and began walking down the aisles, looking for the Devils and Witchcraft section. The first aisle he walked down was history, the next children's books, and the one after that thriller. It struck him as a weird order to have the sections in, but what did he know about libraries? He had never been in one before.

Scott walked between the bookshelves, filled with thousands of different books, all different colors and sizes. Every few aisles, he would pass a section of tables for patrons to sit and read at. Some of the chairs were pulled out, and books sat open on the tables, but no one was reading them. It was like everyone had disappeared.

After what felt like an hour of searching, Scott finally found the section he was looking for. He looked in the book once more, examining the spine, and began searching the shelf for a second copy of the book, one that wouldn't be missing pages. He ran his fingers over the books as he searched desperately. A memory almost came back to him. It was right on the edge of his mind, but he couldn't make it out. Something he had forgotten.

He searched the bottom two shelves, and the three above that. The book wasn't there. He searched the other side, still holding out hope he would find it. He checked and double-checked, but the book wasn't there.

Scott backed against a shelf and slid down to the floor. It wasn't there. And if it wasn't there, that meant he couldn't—

Wait. Scott noticed a paper sticking up slightly from in between two books. Scott stood up and walked to it, pulling it out. Scott held his breath as he looked at the paper, coarse and yellow, with thick blotches of black ink, and strange symbols written on it.

Scott jumped back in fear and hit the bookshelf as he heard a voice speak from behind him.

"You can't bring them back, Scott," Vincent said as the missing pages in Scott's hand burned like charcoal, the ashes falling from his hands.

Scott's heart pounded in his chest like a hammer as he turned to face Vincent, who was standing in front of him. The light above him began to flicker as Vincent stepped closer, backing him up against the bookshelf.

"Why would you do that?" Scott asked, his voice harsh.

"Because I told you, Scott, there is no way out of this. No happy ending, no escape. Not for you."

"How?" Scott asked. "How did you come back?"

Vincent kept silent for a moment, examining Scott's face. It was time.

"When you and *Dr. Freeman*"—there was spite in his voice as he said that name—"killed me, it didn't work. Not the way it was supposed to, at least." Vincent leaned down closer. "You see, Scott," he growled, "your little procedure didn't kill me, not completely. I stayed alive, buried in your subconscious."

Scott was startled by Vincent's voice. He had never heard it this loud.

"I rotted in your head, alone, for *seven years*! Seven years without holding my wife, or seeing my children's faces. Seven years alone, because you got *scared*!"

"I didn't kill you!"

"You didn't because you couldn't," Vincent growled. "You knew you couldn't kill your other personality, so you went to Dr. Freeman and got him to do it for you."

Scott was shaking. His lungs wouldn't take a breath, and his head felt dizzy. "Why didn't the procedure work?"

"I have no idea," Vincent replied. "But if I had to guess, it probably had something to do with it not being the first time someone tried it." He watched Scott closely, trying to catch his reaction. He had hoped to see surprise on his face, but there was none. All the anger went out of Vincent's voice for the briefest moment. "So you did know."

Scott remained silent. There was nothing to say.

Vincent continued, his voice returning to his normal whisper tone. "Then, one day, I came back. I don't know how, but I did."

"In the car," Scott said, the memory returning to him. "You came back in the car."

Vincent continued, "But I knew it wouldn't last. I knew I had to figure out some way to stay, to survive. That's when I remembered taking April here when she was younger, how she used to sit at the tables reading for hours, and how I looked over the bookshelves while she did." He looked down at the book in Scott's hand. "I remembered seeing that book on the shelf one day, thinking it strange."

"You checked it out," Scott said, piecing it together as the full memory came back to him. The headache in the car, the blackout, the time on the car clock moving forward over two hours. "You drove to the library, and then back to the road, and then you cut my brakes after you did the spell to bring yourself back. Why would you cut my brakes?"

Vincent sighed to himself. "To kill you, Scott."

"Why? If you already had the book, why would you try to kill me? Unless—" His words cut off in an instant as he realized.

"I thought I could kill you, take your place. Be with my family again. That was before I knew what it would to do me, what it would turn me into." In an instant, Vincent's eyes turned black, as cold and lifeless as the crows', before returning to normal. "It brought me back, but as something else. I couldn't be with them like this. Not as this thing, this monster, that you turned me into."

"So you kill them, just to punish me?"

"*Yes!*" Vincent screamed. "I kill them! So that you know what it's like to be all alone, to have everything you love stripped away from you." Vincent's voice cracked and he pushed Scott against the bookshelf, his hand twitching.

"I won't let you hurt them," Scott said. "I'll kill you first."

Vincent smiled. Scott had said *kill*. "True colors revealed at last. Unfortunately for them, you have no idea how to kill me. And even if you did"—Vincent's last words were spoken harshly—"I don't think you have the stomach for it."

Vincent took a moment to calm himself before continuing with pain in his voice. "You took everything, Scott, and I had to live every day for seven years knowing that it was my brother who took them from me. Do you know what that felt like?"

Brother. The word took Scott by surprise. Despite years of talking back and forth through Post-it notes and letters, despite both being trapped in a cage and falling in love with the same woman, loving the same kids, Scott had never thought of Vincent as his brother.

"How did you make Tommy kill May?"

Vincent glared as his eyes turned black. "Like I said, it made me something else."

Scott recognized the black eyes now. The same black eyes Tommy had had when Scott had found him with a knife in his hand. "Why?" he asked. "Why make him kill her? Why not do it yourself?"

"You say they're your kids. Why wouldn't they take after you?"

"I didn't kill you," Scott said.

"You told Dr. Freeman what I had done. You convinced him to do the procedure. You left me there, alone, for seven years."

Vincent tried to stop his hand from twitching as he spoke. "But that's what you do. You leave people."

"That's not true."

"Yes, it is. Because deep down, you're still that scared little kid trapped in the cage, thinking the world is out to get him. Unable to trust anyone, because sooner or later, everyone will remind you of that piece of trash who took you!"

Scott shook his head, but deep down he wondered if Vincent was right.

"That's why you left me to die. That's why you left Tommy alone in the house, knowing that something was wrong with him. And that's why I knew that if I put that book in Karen's drawer, you would leave her too."

Karen. Scott hadn't realized. What had he done?

"You can't save them, Scott!" Vincent screamed as Scott ran for the exit.

Sccrrreeeee

As Scott ran, he heard the scraping. Talons digging into wood, and bone, and flesh. He ran past the tables, seeing people sitting in the chairs, their corpses rotted, crows sitting atop them, picking at their flesh. The stench made his stomach turn as he saw the lady sitting at the desk, a crow picking out her teeth with its beak. As he ran to the door, he heard Vincent's voice echoing behind him.

"You can't save her, Scott. You can't save any of them. There is no escape, no way out. I know everything you've ever been afraid of. This is your nightmare, Scott.

"I am your nightmare!"

Chapter Eighteen

6:05 a.m.

Scott practically leaped out of the car as he sped it into his driveway, running across the front porch to the door. He reached to open it, but the handle was locked. He frantically reached inside his pockets for the keys, almost dropping them as his hands shook wildly. Finally he found the right one and put it in the keyhole, but nothing changed. The door remained locked.

Scott beat against the door with his shoulder, desperately trying to reach Karen, to save her. His shoulder burned like fire as it crashed against the door, once, twice, a dozen times, but he couldn't get in. He screamed for her, hoping she could hear him through the door, but there was no response. What if it was too late? What if she was already dead?

No, he screamed to himself. *Don't think like that. She has to be alive. She has to.*

He began kicking the door, the sound of his shoe crashing into the wood echoing into the street. The sun was beating down on him before the clouds grew in the sky, now blocking the sun.

6:09

At last, the door slammed open, and he ran into the house, crying out for Karen. But there was no answer. He searched the living room but found nothing. Nothing was out of the ordinary, aside from a streak of dirt on the floor, and Tommy's body lying dead in the corner, covered by a sheet. Scott cried out again, desperately holding out hope that she was alive. He couldn't lose her, not like this. He had promised to keep her safe, to protect her from Vincent.

Scott ran to the stairs, seeing dirt stains leading up them. He sprinted up the steps, almost tripping over himself. "Karen!" he pleaded into the silence. His cries went unanswered as he struggled to breathe. He felt lightheaded at the thought of it. He had to find her. But what if he did and it was too late? What if she died before he told her how sorry he was—for accusing her, for Vincent, for everything?

Scott opened the first door, seeing that the room was empty. May's room. He closed his eyes for a second, trying to focus. He had to find Karen right now. Maybe she was just asleep. Maybe she had just passed out from the stress. Yes, that was it, she had just passed out, he told himself. He went to the next room; it too was empty.

"Karen!" His cries grew weaker as the realization started to hit him. She wasn't answering because she couldn't. Vincent had done something to her. He would walk into a room and see her lying in a pool of her own blood, her eyes glazed over.

"Karen!"

Scott slammed open the third door, forcing himself to look despite his fears of what he might find. Would he find a horde of crows tearing into her flesh? Would he find her body hung from the ceiling fan, a rope coiled around her neck like a boa constrictor? Or would she be lying on the bed, choking on her own blood? His eyes examined the room as the door swung open. Tommy's room. Empty.

6:13

In Scott's panic, he hadn't noticed the small pile of dirt underneath the door at the end of the hallway. That was where she must be. He ran over to it, finding it locked. He beat on it, screaming her name, but there was no answer. *She's dead, and it's your fault because you left her*, he told himself as he rammed his shoulder into the door again and again until finally it opened. His mouth was as dry as sandpaper, and his knees felt like loose gravel, as he looked into the room. Joey's room.

6:15

Karen sat in the corner of the room next to Joey's crib. Dirt covered her feet and hands, and she didn't look up at him,

instead staring at the floor, staring through the floor, her hair covering her face. She was alive.

Scott ran over to her, hugging her without thinking. He felt the coarse dirt against his skin as it rubbed off on him. It was in her hair, too. He looked over her for a moment, making sure she wasn't bleeding or injured in any way. She wasn't.

"Karen," he said as he touched her cheek with his hands. She was alive. Nothing else mattered to him in that moment, even the words she was muttering under her breath.

"Wouldn't stop."

6:16

As he looked at her, he breathed a sigh of relief. In that moment, a bomb could have gone off behind him and he wouldn't have noticed. All he saw was his wife, alive. But when he looked into her eyes, his lungs stopped. Her black eyes.

"Karen?" he asked when, in a moment, her eyes returned to normal. He pushed the hair out of her face as she looked up at him, confused.

"Scott?" she asked as she looked around the room, trying to get her bearings. "How did I get here?"

"You don't remember?"

She shook her head.

He hesitated, but he had to tell her. "I think you blacked out like Tommy did. Try—try to remember what happened."

Karen thought, her eyes still partially glazed over, like when you wake up suddenly from a deep sleep. "I don't know. I was

mad at you when you left, and scared. And then—then Joey started crying. I-I thought if Vincent came back before you did, then he would find us. I had to get Joey to stop crying. But—but he wouldn't stop."

A terrifying realization spread over Scott in an instant as he looked into Joey's crib to find only the blanket lying inside. "Karen," he asked softly as he turned back to her. "Where's Joey?"

"I don't know," she said as she twisted her head, trying to think. Her voice was breaking up. "He wouldn't stop crying. I had to—I had to get him to stop crying. I think—I think I—" She almost gagged at the next word. "Oh, no."

"What, what did you—" His words cut off in horror as he looked at his wife, covered with dirt. Coarse brown dirt, the kind you find six feet below the surface. Dirt from the backyard.

6:17

Scott was frozen in horror, but only for a moment. He darted out of the room, practically falling down the stairs as he took them four at a time. Karen was close behind. He saw the dirt in the living room as he passed it, tripping over himself as he ran. He couldn't feel his legs anymore; the only thing keeping him standing was the faintest hope that he was wrong.

Scott tore through the kitchen, catching a glimpse of the backyard out of the window. He didn't accept what he saw. It was just a fleeting glance. Maybe he had seen it wrong. Maybe it wasn't a shovel.

Dirt was tracked through the kitchen, leading to the back door. He had been running, but the sight of the backyard stopped him in his tracks as his feet hit the grass.

Karen couldn't follow him out. The sight was too much for her. She collapsed in the doorway, biting her lip and weeping hopelessly, knowing what she had done.

Scott forced himself to step closer to it, but his feet felt like concrete. He felt like he could pass out, almost wanted to, to avoid the truth a little while longer, but he was afforded no such luxury. He stepped closer to the shovel.

It stuck out of the ground, its blade stabbed into the grass. Its wooden shaft was covered in dirt, and Scott felt his entire body go numb from the shock.

His legs gave out, and he collapsed to his knees as he reached it. The shovel, and the small pile of brown dirt that sat next to it. The pile that tore into his heart worse than a thousand crows. The pile was small, but big enough to cover it up. The hole that Karen had dug.

The grave where she'd buried their eight-month-old son.

Alive.

Chapter Nineteen

Vincent had just finished a shower and was putting on a two-piece suit. He was going out with Karen tonight, and he was nervous. He knew what the right thing to do was, and he had tried so many times, but could never bring himself to do it. As he checked his reflection in the mirror, he saw the Post-it note.

Tell her.

Vincent sighed deeply. Scott was right. It wasn't right to keep lying to her. But how could he tell her the truth, who he really was? He couldn't bear to see the look on her face. The look of fear she would give him. Vincent pulled the note off and opened the medicine cabinet, where he kept his comb. Inside was another note.

Don't ignore me.

He laughed to himself. He knew Scott meant well, but he didn't understand how hard it was. Scott didn't have anything to hide, anything to be ashamed of. She wouldn't look at Scott differently the way she would look at him.

Vincent pulled the note down as he grabbed his comb. He combed his hair more loosely than Scott did. As he set the

comb down and began brushing his teeth, he found another note in the toothbrush holder.

Good luck.

Easy for him to say.

P.S. I ate all of our ice cream.

Vincent smiled. "I'm gonna kill him."

Karen sat on the bridge, waiting for Scott to show up. It was late at night, and the moon was shining down from the sky, shimmering over the lake beneath her. Her roommate had insisted on taking a picture of her before she left, despite her protests. You'll never forget your first dance with him, the roommate had said. However, she wasn't planning on going to the dance. She disliked parties, and she and Scott had decided to skip it in favor of walking around the city. The lights shined from the buildings in the distance, looking like stars hanging low in the sky.

The bridge was on the edge of the city, and at this time of night, there was practically no one in sight. Good; she also disliked large crowds. But standing there in the middle of the night, it began to get unnerving. Especially since Scott was running late.

Vincent waited behind the trees, a few dozen feet away. He had been standing there over thirty minutes, trying to convince himself not to tell her. She didn't have to know. She would just look at him like everyone else. Maybe she should.

Vincent didn't deny what he was. He knew there was a reason that Dr. Freeman looked at him that way, a reason

everyone did. Maybe he should tell her, let her leave. Maybe she would be safer.

"Boo," Karen said as she snuck up behind him, startling him.

Vincent jumped back slightly. He knew it was her, but he hadn't expected her to see him. He should tell her right now, he decided. Get it over with quick. But look at her. She was wearing a sleeveless navy-blue dress, with two-inch white heels. Her hair was parted on the right side, falling down her back like a waterfall, with a strand covering her right eye. She had earrings, gold ones in the shape of flowers, her favorite ones. She had gotten dressed up for this date. How could he ruin it for her? *She dressed up for Scott*, he reminded himself. *You have to tell her.*

"Were you planning on hiding behind this tree all night?" she asked, giggling. "I mean, it is a pretty nice tree."

Vincent laughed with her. He wanted the words to come out, but they wouldn't. He didn't want her to stop laughing, didn't want to scare her.

"What were you doing back here?" Karen asked, half-joking.

"Oh, just nervous about the date, I guess."

"Why?" she asked. "It's not like we haven't gone out before."

"You're right, I guess I'm just nervous." Vincent hated changing his voice to sound like Scott. Just another way he lied to her.

"Well, come on," she said, grabbing his hand and pulling him towards the bridge.

He smiled and followed her.

"So, where do you want to go?" she asked as they walked.

"Up to you," Vincent said, barely hearing her. The longer he waited, the worse it would be. How could he keep lying to her? It was driving him crazy. So was her jet-black hair, glowing in the moonlight. He couldn't tell her. Not tonight.

"Well, I think the zoo is open late. We can stop by there again," she said as they approached the bridge. "I bet the animals look even better at night."

Again. The words stung like fire. She was talking about a date he hadn't been on. He couldn't do this anymore. It was wrong.

"You okay?" she asked as they walked across the bridge.

Vincent stopped walking halfway, forcing the words to come out. "I'm sorry." His voice was nervous, and he looked down at the ground. "I wanted to do this earlier, when we weren't alone, so—so you wouldn't be scared."

She looked at him, her eyebrow rising. "Scott, what's wrong?"

"My—" Vincent felt the words would choke him as they left his mouth. "My name's not Scott."

She laughed, not realizing what he was saying. "You gave me a fake name?" she asked almost sarcastically.

"It's not a fake name," he said, still keeping Scott's voice without realizing it. Despite going over this conversation in his head a thousand times, now that he was standing in front of her, he didn't know how to explain it. "When you went to the zoo, the one who went with you, his name was Scott. My name—my name isn't."

Karen laughed, still thinking it was a joke. "What, you got a twin brother, and you swap out girlfriends in between dates?" She laughed for another moment before realizing he wasn't joking. "That's not it, is it?"

Vincent shook his head. "No, no, of course not."

"Then what are you talking about?" There was genuine concern in her voice.

"It's..." He struggled to find the words. "When Scott was young..."

"You were kidnapped," she interrupted. "Locked in a cage for almost three months. You already told me that."

"Did Scott tell you how he escaped?"

"'You told me that your therapist found you and called the cops." She hesitated for a moment before continuing. "But that was a lie."

Vincent tilted his head, shocked.

"I felt you weren't telling me everything, so I researched it myself. It wasn't that hard. It was all over the papers where you grew up. Your therapist did find you, but the man was already dead."

Vincent looked up from the ground, but not at her. Never at her.

"I know you killed him, Scott. Is that what this is about?"

"Yes—no. No, it's not," he said, grinding his teeth, forcing the words out. "About a month after Scott was taken, he tried to run away. He got pretty far, but then the man found him. Beat him. That's the first thing I remember."

Her mouth opened slightly as she realized. "Scott had DID. You're another personality."

Vincent nodded.

Karen stood quiet, everything sinking in at once. After a few minutes had passed, she finally spoke. "So you're not Scott?" she asked, already knowing the answer. "How do you switch?"

Vincent stood for a second, shocked by her question. "We switch at night, when we go to sleep."

"Okay, so it's every other day?" Karen asked. "Can you do it awake, if you want to?"

"Yes, but we don't. It's—it's different."

"Okay," she said plainly. "Why didn't you tell me this before?"

Vincent was surprised. He had expected her to react differently, react worse. He wanted to look at her, really look, but couldn't bring himself to.

"Did you think I would leave if I knew?" Her voice almost sounded hurt. "I mean, I admit it, it's different, but it's not Scott's fault for being taken." She saw the look on Vincent's face. "Or your fault for existing."

He almost looked at her before stopping himself. She didn't know everything. "But, you don't understand, I didn't just show up. I-I killed the man. I killed him." He returned to looking at the ground, ashamed.

"So," she said. "The man took an eight-year-old boy. Locked you up for months. It didn't bother me when I thought Scott did it. Why would it bother me that you did?"

Vincent paused. He didn't know what to say. She wasn't nervous, wasn't running away.

"What's your name?" she asked.

After a moment of silence, the word came out in his own voice. "Vincent."

"Have we met before, Vincent?"

She wasn't startled by his voice. Didn't seem scared. "Yes. Several times. I was at the—"

"The park?" she asked.

"Yes, how did you—"

Karen smiled. "Because you didn't look at me then either. What are you afraid of?"

Vincent knew he had to. It wasn't fair to her to keep prolonging it. She would see what he was. He looked up, into her eyes, and held his breath.

She didn't shudder. Didn't back away. Instead, she smiled and stepped closer to him. "Was that so hard?"

She wasn't afraid. Vincent didn't understand. No one had ever not been afraid.

Karen knew what he was thinking. She could read it on his face. "Why would I be scared of you?"

"Most people are," Vincent said quietly.

"So?" She shrugged. "Do you know why it didn't bother me when I thought Scott killed that man?"

Vincent shook his head.

"Because despite knowing that, I still felt safe with him. I knew he wouldn't hurt me." She stepped closer to him, now barely a foot apart. "I feel safe with you too."

"You're not scared?" he asked, his heart rate quickening.

"No, I'm not."

They both stood quietly, letting everything sink in.

Vincent looked at her. Not around her, but at her, for the first time. She was so beautiful. She didn't shudder, didn't look at him differently. Instead, she moved closer.

Karen's mind was going back over the dates they had had, realizing which ones were Vincent. "Wait," she said softly. "If it was you at the park, and you at the—" She stopped. "That means we haven't..."

Vincent shook his head, never taking his eyes off hers.

Karen stepped closer until they were inches apart. The moon was reflecting off her hair, and the sound of the water crashing underneath the bridge filled the night sky, but Vincent couldn't hear it.

He could barely breathe. He could feel goose bumps on his skin as he watched her lean in slightly. She had goose bumps too.

Vincent leaned in, sliding his hand up her back and into her hair as he kissed her. For the first time in his life, he didn't feel alone.

Thirteen months later, Scott proposed to Karen, followed by Vincent the next night. She said yes to both.

Two years after that, Karen gave birth to April with Scott by her side. Then, when night came and everyone had gone to sleep, Vincent woke up.

Vincent woke up in a chair on the right side of the hospital bed that Karen was lying in. He watched her sleep for a moment but then turned to the crib that was lying in the corner of the room.

Hospitals typically take the baby to the nursery for the night, while the parents sleep, but Scott had requested that she be left in the room. He didn't want Vincent to have to wait until morning to see her.

Vincent stood up quietly so as not to wake Karen and walked over to April, lying in her crib asleep. He smiled as he saw her for the first time. She looked so much like her mother. He leaned down and picked her up, careful not to wake her.

He carried her back to his chair, rocking her softly in his arms before sitting back down beside Karen.

He rocked her in his arms for hours, never taking his eyes off of her. She was so beautiful, so innocent. He promised her in that moment that he would never let anything happen to her.

Suddenly, April woke up. Vincent was startled; he didn't want her to cry, to wake Karen up. But she didn't. She looked up at Vincent, right into his eyes, and giggled. He smiled back at her as she raised her hand and grabbed his thumb before going back to sleep. She wasn't scared either.

Morning came and Karen woke up, looking over at Vincent still holding April. "She reminds me of you," she said, smiling at him as he carried their baby to her.

Karen took April in her arms as Vincent knelt down over them, kissing her on the cheek. He looked back and forth between them as she began singing softly to April. Her singing voice was slightly off-key, but he didn't notice. It sounded perfect. Like her. Vincent smiled as he looked down at April.

Like both of them.

Chapter Twenty

April was nine years old when the dreams came back.

Vincent woke up, sweat pouring down his face as he shot up in the bed. Karen heard his breathing from the next room and rushed in to see what was wrong.

"Are you okay?" she asked as she leaned over the bed to him.

He tried to slow his breathing as he responded, "I'm fine, just a bad dream." He could feel his heart pounding inside his chest, like it was trying to crawl out.

She sat down on the bed beside him, putting her arm around his back. "Scott told me that you've been having the dreams a lot recently."

Vincent didn't know what to say. He had been having them a lot recently, but the truth was he had never really stopped, not like Scott had. Scott's dreams were about fear, and they had gone away with therapy from Dr. Freeman. But his were different. They weren't about fear; they were about longing, craving something, something that had never truly gone away.

"You hurt people in them, don't you?" she asked, her voice not afraid but curious.

"Yes."

"Do you ever hurt us?" It wouldn't have mattered to her what the answer was; she just wanted to see if he would tell her.

"No," Vincent said immediately, holding her cheek with his hand. "Not once, I swear. I would never."

"I know," she said, touching her hand to his before reaching behind him and hitting him on the back of the head with a pillow. "Now get up, the kids are getting ready for school."

Vincent laughed as he got out of bed.

Downstairs, the kids had almost finished eating when Vincent walked into the living room. Dakota jumped up on his leg and he leaned down to pet him. "Good dog," he said as Dakota wagged his tail violently.

"Come here," May said, only two years old at the time. Dakota ran to her, almost knocking her out of her chair.

"I got you," Vincent said as he steadied the chair with his hand before leaning down and kissing her on the cheek.

"Time for school," Karen said as she walked into the room.

"Aww," April and Tommy cried in unison.

"Why can't we stay home?" April asked. "We'll be good."

"That's not a very compelling argument," Vincent said before turning to Karen. "What do you think? Should they stay home?"

"I don't think so," she said as she gathered up their backpacks.

"Aww, come on, Mom," April added, using puppy eyes.

Vincent knelt down behind April, imitating her sad eyes to Karen. "Yeah, come on, Mom."

"Cute," she said, smirking.

"Aww, she's no fun," Vincent said as he turned his head toward April. "She is right, though. School is important."

"But I already know everything," she said, desperate.

"Really? What's nine times fifty-two?"

"Four hundred and sixty-eight," April said immediately.

Vincent was surprised by her speed. "Okay, what's four thousand, three hundred and seventy-one divided by forty-seven?"

"Ninety-three," she said, smiling up at him.

"Well played," he said as he grabbed her backpack from Karen. "But you still have to go."

"Why?" she pleaded. Tommy had already accepted his fate and was putting his shoes on, but April was still resistant.

"I'll tell you what," he said as he smiled at her. "If you go to school today, you can stay home tomorrow."

"Really?" she asked.

"Yep."

"Thanks, Dad," she said, hugging him on his side while she put her backpack on. She ran through the kitchen and out the door, joining Tommy as they waited for the bus.

Vincent would never forget what that hug felt like.

"She didn't realize tomorrow is Saturday?" Karen asked him.

"Nope."

"How?" Karen asked. "She's the smartest kid we got."

"Easy," Vincent said as he walked towards the living room window. "Once I told her she could stay home, she thought she had won and stopped paying attention to the details."

"That's a pretty important detail," she joked.

"Not when you aren't looking for it," he said. "Besides, in time, I feel she'll come to forgive me."

Vincent was watching them out the window as they waited for the bus. Tommy was trying to poke April while she wasn't looking, or tug on her ponytail. April was planning her next break-in to his room, to attack him with pillows. She got that from her mother.

"Play hide-and-seek?" May asked as she stepped toward Vincent in the living room.

"Sure," he said as he took his eyes off the window and knelt down in front of her. He covered his eyes for a moment and then started counting. He continued to count but opened his eyes after a few seconds, knowing she was long gone, probably hiding in a corner, covering her eyes. She thought if she couldn't see him, he couldn't see her. He looked down the hallway, smiling, when the clock struck 6:17, and their lives were changed forever.

"Help!"

Vincent heard Tommy scream. He looked out the window to see Tommy standing helplessly on the sidewalk as April was being pulled into a white car he had never seen before. He saw April's horrified expression as she tried to fight, to pull away, but to no avail. The hands of the stranger pulled her in. Into the dark shadow of the car. Out of Vincent's sight.

Vincent was out of the door before Tommy finished screaming the word, but it was too late. By the time he reached the sidewalk, the car had vanished across the street, taking April with it. He stood on the sidewalk, not knowing what to do. He heard Karen crying as she watched from the doorway, but his body sat frozen in disbelief as he looked onto the empty street where his daughter had been taken from him. For the first time in over ten years, he felt alone.

You let them take her, Vincent told himself. *Why didn't you watch her? Why didn't you do something? You promised her.*

"Sir?" the detective said.

Vincent and Karen sat in the office of the lead detective at the police station. It had been two hours since April had been taken, and the cops were already tracking down the car, but so far, no luck. The detective wanted to question the parents to see if they had noticed anything specific, something that might help in the search.

"Yes?" Vincent said, snapping out of his thoughts.

"I asked you if you noticed anything about the suspects, anything that might help us. You already gave the cop on duty a description of the car, and we are trying, but we will need to identify them when we find it."

He thought for a moment as Karen spoke, fighting back the tears. "We only got a brief glance. I didn't have time to see anything."

"That's okay," the detective said. "In situations like this, it's common for people, especially parents, to be so focused on their kids, they don't notice anything else."

As he finished the sentence, a sketch artist walked in with a yellow pad and pen in hand.

"Anything you can tell us," the detective asked Vincent. "It's okay if you can't. I understand it was just a brief glance."

Vincent had the picture in his head. "Two men, both Caucasian. The first had a burr haircut, brown, and a cut above his right eye, about two inches long. He weighed two thirty, maybe two thirty-five. He had a silver watch on his left wrist, partially covering up a tattoo. I think it was a zodiac sign. It had horns, probably Aries. His face was wide, and his complexion was dark, very tan."

The detective looked on with wide eyes as he continued.

"The other man was smaller, probably around one forty-five. He had longer hair, blond. He had a heart tattoo on his shoulder, and what looked like a gold tooth. He looked out of breath, either smoking or asthma, and his hand had a crescent-shaped cut across the wrist."

The sketch artist showed Vincent the picture he had drawn, and Vincent took it from him. "No, it's more like this," he said as he drew on the pad.

"You get their height too?" the detective joked.

"The first was five-nine and the second six-two."

"They were in a car," the sketch artist rebutted.

Vincent said nothing as he turned the notepad back around.

The cop looked at it in amazement. He had practically drawn a photograph of the two men—men he couldn't have looked at for more than two seconds. "Okay," the detective said as he took the drawings. "We'll look into it."

The words didn't calm Vincent. His lungs felt like they would collapse in his chest as his heart pounded like a bulldozer. How could he let them take her? She was probably locked up somewhere, just like he had been. He couldn't bear to think of her going through that. He was supposed to keep her safe.

He'd promised.

It was eleven days before they found her.

When the cops brought her home, she had scars all over her body. They said most would heal in time, but that didn't matter to Vincent as he saw his daughter crying, shaking as she walked into the house. He ran over to her, to hug her, but she moved away at his touch.

"April?" Vincent asked as he bent down in front of her. His heart broke when he saw the fear in her eyes as she looked back into his.

"Where were you?" she asked, her head twitching as she looked side to side, still uneasy, thinking the men would show back up at any second.

Vincent knew she didn't mean it, that she was still in shock, but it didn't matter. She was right. He hadn't been there. Not when she'd needed him. He couldn't protect his own daughter. For the first time, his daughter was scared of him.

One week later

April woke up screaming from a nightmare. Scott rushed into her room, seeing her sweating on the edge of her bed. He ran to her, seeing her expression, the one that had been on his face for too many years. Seeing the fear on his daughter's face,

knowing that she had been taken the same as him, was too much for him. He didn't know how to handle it.

He took her in his arms as she cried onto his chest. Karen came to the door, but he motioned her to go back to bed. He would stay with his daughter. He needed to stay with his daughter.

Scott could feel her shaking as she cried, the same way he had shaken when he was first rescued. He wanted to say something to her but didn't know what. How could he tell her he was sorry? How could he tell her that he wouldn't let it happen again? He hadn't even been there when it had happened. He should have been.

The next morning, after breakfast, Karen drove the kids to school. Scott was alone in the house, getting ready for work, when the kitchen phone rang.

"Hello?"

"Hi, Scott," the detective on the other line said. "I'm afraid I have some bad news."

"What is it?"

"They let them go," the detective said. "I'm sorry."

"What? Why!" Scott howled into the phone.

"There wasn't enough evidence on them to hold them."

"How can there not be enough evidence? You found her in their apartment. You found her blood on their walls."

"Okay, Scott," the detective said. "I didn't want you to find out this way, but their lawyer pulled up your old records. They know about you being taken when you were a child, you killing the man, and your mental illness."

"What's that have to do with anything!?"

"They were found and arrested on the basis of an eyewitness, that eyewitness being you. Due to your illness, it is inadmissible as evidence, and since it was the grounds for their arrest, their lawyer had arranged for them to be let go. It's just temporary," he added, but Scott had already dropped the phone.

How could they let them go? They'd be halfway across the country before it went to trial. How could they do this? Because of the mental illness. Because of Vincent.

The stress was too much for Scott. Before he realized what was happening, his head began to hurt. Hurt bad. Somehow, Vincent had heard the phone call.

"No," Scott said as his head burned in fire. He leaned over, bracing himself on the counter, as his head twisted violently. Vincent was forcing a change. "Please, don't," Scott said, trying to fight. He knew what Vincent would do. "No," he said once more before screaming in pain. He writhed as he held on to the counter, his right hand beginning to twitch. In a moment, it was over, and the room fell silent.

Vincent rose from the bar slowly, tilting his head slightly sideways. He took a deep, slow breath, the only thing that could be heard through the silence of the house, before turning toward the door. As he walked, he reached over and grabbed a long silver knife from the knife block. As he pulled it out, the block fell over onto the floor, chipping the side. The other knives spilled out of it.

Vincent flipped the knife backwards in his hand and held it tight. As he stepped out the door, his right hand began to shake.

It was well after noon when Karen walked back into the house, carrying a bag of groceries; she had had several errands to run after dropping the kids off at school.

The door was unlocked. Strange, Scott usually locked it when he left for work. She thought nothing of it until she saw the knives spilled out over the kitchen floor. She dropped the groceries and went to the living room, grabbing the shotgun they kept hidden behind the cabinet, the one they had bought after April was taken. She cocked it and looked around the house, noticing a drop of blood on the stairs. She followed it up, holding the gun up in front of her. When she reached the top of the stairs, she saw the blood trail leading into their bedroom.

She walked down the hallway, pushing the cracked door open with the barrel of the gun, and stepped inside. Blood stained the white shag carpet, and she walked carefully into the room. The blood led towards the bathroom.

The door was open, and Karen slowly walked to it, holding her breath. She didn't know what—who could be in there. The police had called her and told her about letting the men go. Maybe they had come back and broken into the house. She stepped in front of the door and dropped the shotgun, which landed on the bloodstained carpet, as she saw the bathtub completely covered in blood, and Vincent sitting inside it.

Vincent was still wearing his clothes, which were soaked in blood as well. He was twitching his head back and forth erratically as Karen walked over to him. She didn't have to ask what he had done. She didn't even have to ask which one he was. She knew. She always knew.

She knelt down beside him as he looked down at his hands, trying to wipe the blood off, but with nothing to wipe it with. It was his way to look at his hands instead of her. He couldn't look at her like this.

"Vincent," she said softly. "Are you okay?"

"I-I couldn't. I couldn't stop. I tried, but—but it was too much. I had to." His voice was more broken than Karen had ever heard it. "I wanted to."

"It's okay," she said as she touched her hand to his cheek, but he pulled away.

"Don't," he said. "You need to leave. Get as far away as you can. I don't know—I don't know what I'll do."

She watched him shaking with fear for the first time in his life. "I'm not going to leave you." She saw him look at the floor, ashamed, before she took his head in her hands, pulling it up to face her. "Look at me," she whispered softly as his eyes met hers. Even covered in blood, she didn't flinch when he looked at her. "Do I look afraid?"

A tear fell down Vincent's face, making a line in the blood. "Maybe you should be."

She smiled. "Never."

Vincent sat there for a moment, covered in blood, as she got a towel and began wiping the blood off his face.

"I didn't mean it," Vincent stammered. "I didn't."

"I know," she said.

Suddenly, Vincent grunted in pain as his head jerked forward. Before she could help, the pain stopped, and Scott looked up at her.

"Karen?" he said. "I was—I got a call. They said they were letting them go."

She looked at Scott with sympathy. He was dazed; he hadn't noticed the blood yet. She feared how he would react.

"Then, it went black. Vincent was—" His memory returned to him. "Vincent took over. I could feel him. He was going to do something." Scott looked down, seeing the blood for the first time. It was covering everything, but he had been too distracted to notice until now. He felt it on his skin, saw it on the wall, the blood he had seen so many times in Vincent's dreams.

"What did he do?" Scott asked. "What did he do!"

A few days later, Scott walked into the therapist's office for his monthly session.

"Hello, Scott," Dr. Freeman greeted him. "It's nice to see you."

Scott nodded before pacing the floor.

"I heard about April," Dr. Freeman said, noticing him pacing. "I'm truly sorry. I would have called, but since you didn't contact me, I thought it might be best to leave you to your family. If I can help in any way—"

"I need to talk to you about something."

"Anything," he replied.

"It's about Vincent."

Dr. Freeman thought this over for a moment before responding. "What about him?"

"A few months ago, his dreams started coming back."

Dr. Freeman nodded. "He told me."

"Yeah, well, I thought he had it under control. He had had these dreams before and, outside of the man who took us, he never acted on it. But now..."

"Now what?"

"The men who took April, they were let go by the cops because it was Vincent's description that got them arrested, and due to our mental illness, it was thrown out as evidence to arrest them."

"That's absurd," Dr. Freeman stated. "Surely it won't stick."

"That's the thing. It doesn't matter anymore. Vincent," Scott stammered, "Vincent found them."

"My word," Dr. Freeman said. He knew what that meant.

"I remember bits and pieces of it," Scott said as his head twisted with disgust. "The things he did to them. Horrible things."

Dr. Freeman closed his eyes and tried to think. This was what he had always feared, Vincent slipping, going down the rabbit hole and not coming back. Now maybe he was lost forever. "Maybe it was an isolated incident." He was trying to convince himself more than he was Scott.

"No," Scott said. "The dreams were back before. And they have gotten worse. I can feel him, even now. That dark part of him trying to claw its way out."

"What about the cops? Surely you'll be a suspect in the murders."

"You know Vincent, how he thinks. He could've murdered them in the courtroom and found a way to get out of it. He's smart like that."

"I suppose you're right," Dr. Freeman said. "But I'm still wondering what you propose we do."

"If Vincent loses control again, if he gives in, I can't trust that he wouldn't hurt Karen. Or the kids."

"Do you really think he could go that far, to murder someone he cares about? Killing these men is one thing, but killing Karen, killing the kids? That is something else entirely."

"You told me a long time ago that the man who kidnapped me had gotten better, but once he slipped, there was no coming back. Once he broke, there was no fixing him."

"Yes, but this is different. You're not talking about kidnapping a kid, or killing some random stranger. This is his family. To do that, it wouldn't just take a slip. He would have to be broken. Shattered completely."

"How long until that happens?" Scott asked. "How can I know it won't be tomorrow, or next month or next year? When he does, I won't be able to stop him."

"Are you suggesting what I think you are?" Dr. Freeman responded uneasily.

"All I know is that I can't risk him hurting Karen, or April, or Tommy, or May, or anyone else. I can't take that chance with my family."

Dr. Freeman thought for a moment before answering, his voice careful. "If we do this, there is no going back. Are you sure?"

Scott's hands were shaking from nerves. This felt wrong, but how could he live with himself if Vincent hurt them? He had seen the blood, the same blood Vincent longed for in his dreams. Scott couldn't risk it. Not even for him. "I care about Vincent, I always have. Trust me, this is the last thing I want." His voice was cracking as he spoke, and his eyes began to water. "But tell me, honestly. Have you ever had a patient slip this far back and come out on the other side?"

"No." Dr. Freeman swallowed the lump in his throat. "No, I haven't."

They both stayed silent as Dr. Freeman walked over to his desk, pulling out the bottle of chemicals from the bottom drawer, as well as the jar of liquor from the top. Dr. Freeman poured himself a glass and drank it all at once. He placed the glass back onto the table, grabbed a cup of coffee, and poured the chemical into it. The chemical would put Vincent in a suggestible state, where Dr. Freeman could get rid of him without allowing him to change back to Scott.

Scott sat on the couch, restless. How could he do this to Vincent, after everything? It broke his heart just thinking about it, and here he was, about to do it. But he had to. Even now he could feel Vincent in the back of his mind, thinking about it. The feeling he got while torturing the men. Scott shuddered as he felt it too.

Dr. Freeman put the liquor up and sat back down in his chair. "Scott, before we do this, I have to ask you something."

"Anything."

"Is protecting them the only reason you're doing this?" Before Scott could say yes, he continued. "I mean honestly, have you thought about this, hard? Because if there is any other reason inside you, whether you realize it or not, the guilt will eat you from the inside until there's nothing left."

Scott considered this for a moment before responding. "Yes, I'm sure. I don't want to do this, but Vincent can't come back from this. If he could see it in himself, I think he would say the same thing."

"Okay," Dr. Freeman said, taking a deep breath before nodding for him to do it.

Scott closed his eyes and concentrated. He remembered how he felt in the field, how he switched to Vincent. As he felt himself slipping, his thoughts haunted him. The day he had always feared was here, and he was the one doing it. But it was the only way to protect them. Before he turned, Scott said one last thing. "I'm sorry, Vincent."

Vincent looked up at Dr. Freeman, surprised. "Why am I here?"

Dr. Freeman sat in his chair, holding his notepad on his lap, trying to keep his hands from shaking. "Scott said you were having a hard time with what happened to April and thought it might help for me to talk to you."

"Okay," Vincent said.

"Coffee?" Dr. Freeman offered, motioning to the already poured cup on his desk. "Scott declined, and I hate to waste it."

"Of course," Vincent said. Dr. Freeman got up and brought him the cup. "Thank you."

Dr. Freeman forced a smile and sat back down. "So, Scott tells me April had been having trouble?"

"Yes," Vincent answered.

"What about?"

Vincent struggled to say the words. "Being taken. She screams in her sleep, and I want to help her, but I don't know how. It's like, it's like I can't do anything for her. It feels like I can't protect her anymore."

Dr. Freeman bit his tongue to stop himself from warning him as Vincent raised the cup to his mouth and drank it.

"Strange," Vincent said. "That tastes—" The cup fell out of his hand, shattering on the floor. As he looked at Dr. Freeman,

his mouth began to quiver, and his eyes looked like a dead man's. "Why?"

It broke Dr. Freeman's heart to see him like this. "You know why."

"No," Vincent said as he felt the chemical causing him to slip. "No, you can't, please."

"For what it's worth"—Dr. Freeman paused, holding back the tears—"I never wanted it to end this way."

"Please," Vincent said, "don't take me away from them."

Dr. Freeman did the psychological procedure and, despite how wrong it felt, it was over now. Soon Scott would wake up, and his family would be safe. But one thing still haunted Dr. Freeman. When he was doing the procedure, when Vincent should have been fully unaware, unable to think, unable to move, Vincent's right hand had twitched.

Chapter Twenty-One

Scott sat on the bedroom floor, his back against the wall as he stared into the distance. Karen was in the bathroom with the door shut, trying to wash the dirt off her. The dirt from where she had buried Joey.

How could you let this happen? Scott asked himself. *How could you leave them, leave her, alone?* His eyes watered as he stared blankly at the wall, not knowing what to do. He'd left them, knowing what could happen, just because he had gotten scared, just because he didn't trust her. Maybe Vincent was right.

Vincent. How could he do this? How could he make Karen bury her own child alive? Scott had always known what Vincent was, what he craved, but this was different. This was his family.

His family. The thought stung in Scott's mind. He thought about May, her screams when she'd died, the blood that covered her face. He thought about Tommy, how he'd looked when he'd realized what he had done. The remorse on his face. The same look he had seen on his own face so many years ago.

But he was right. Vincent was a monster; this proved it. To do that to them, to do that to Karen, to Joey. Joey. Scott's throat choked him when he thought of that name. He should have been there. Maybe he could have stopped Karen; maybe things would have been different.

Scott leaned his head back against the wall.

Night had come once more, as moonlight shined through the window. Wind blew in, icy and harsh, sweeping over him, but he didn't notice. Didn't care. His family was dead, and it was his fault. *Why didn't you see the signs sooner?* he asked himself. *Why did you ignore it, chalk it up to no sleep, hallucinations? You knew what Vincent was capable of. Why didn't you stop him?*

Stop him. The words rang in his head as he remembered what Vincent had told him.

"You have no idea how to kill me, and even if you did, I don't think you have the stomach for it."

Vincent had spoken the words in anger, trying to scare him, to rob him of hope. Break him. But now, Scott realized something. Vincent had tripped up in his anger, said something he shouldn't have. It meant there was a way to kill him.

Scott looked over at the book lying on the floor, the book with a red cover and gold lining. He crawled across the floor and picked it up, thumbing through the pages, looking for something. Something to stop Vincent.

He found the place where the pages were ripped out. Where Vincent had found the way to come back in his own body. To come back as something else. He flipped over to the next page. The words were difficult to read, scribbled on the old

parchment with thick, blotchy ink, but he could make it out, just barely. It said something about the spell. Something about how he came back. Scott read the page, his eyes widening with every word. Could this be true? He kept reading, his pulse quickening. This was it.

"April," Scott said to himself.

He set the book down to his side. He had found the answer, found out how to stop him, and Vincent was right—Scott couldn't do it. But neither could he.

Scott heard crying from the bathroom. Karen. He stood up and walked closer to the door, listening to her. She was weeping. It was all he could stand to hear her like this. He wanted to knock on the door, to ask if she was okay, but what could he say to her? Then Scott heard the hammer of the silver revolver click back. The gun fired before he could open the door. He heard the click of the hammer hitting the empty chamber as he rushed in, seeing Karen sitting on the floor with the gun pointed towards her chin.

"No!" Scott screamed as he dove for her, knocking the gun out of her hand as she fired the second shot. The bullet tore through the ceiling, leaving behind it a sound that echoed in the room. But it couldn't drown out her crying.

Her eyes were not black but normal. This was her, what she wanted. Scott held her as she wept in his arms. "It's okay," he said, crying himself as he held her, "It's okay. That's not the answer."

"He killed them, Scott." Karen cried into his arms. "He killed them. How could he do that? After everything, how could he take them from me?"

"I don't know," he whispered back. "I don't know."

"I killed him, I killed our baby."

"No, you didn't," he said as he held her. "No, you didn't."

"They're all dead," she cried.

"Not April," he told her, trying to give her hope.

"He took her and then he killed her," she said. "We both know it."

"No, he didn't," Scott said, and he watched the glimmer of light come back into Karen's eyes. "He couldn't."

"Why?"

"I read the book. I know how he came back. He couldn't just resurrect himself. His body, his soul, is feeding off someone else. It would have to be someone like him, someone he wouldn't kill, because if they die, he dies."

"You think it's April?" she asked, surprised.

"It has to be someone like them for it to work. Who is more like Vincent than April? He would want to keep her safe, make sure she survived. That's why she's the only one he didn't kill. He can't kill her until the end, because once he kills her, it's over. He's saving her for last."

"She's alive," Karen said as she hugged him.

"Yes," he answered. "She's alive."

They both stood up. "How do we save her?" she asked. "We have to save her."

"I don't know," Scott said as he held her, their reflection covering the mirror. "I don't—" His words were cut off when he saw his reflection, bleeding, covered in scars, watching him.

Vincent crashed through the window, glass shattering everywhere. He stepped towards them and threw Karen across

the room towards the mirror. She slammed into it, the broken glass cutting her skin, and landed on the floor, unconscious.

"Hello, Scott," Vincent said as he stepped closer toward him.

"Vincent," Scott said, still in shock, as he backed against the wall.

They looked at each other, at their own twisted reflections, before Scott spoke. "How could you make her do that? How could you make her kill Joey?"

Vincent looked at him, tilting his head. "I told you I would take everything from you."

"That's your excuse," Scott said, surprised at how firm he sounded.

"No, you keep telling yourself that because you don't want to accept the truth. They died because of what you did. Their blood is on your hands."

"Liar," Scott said. "You killed them because you craved it. You made her bury Joey alive, because in your twisted mind, you wanted to."

"I wanted to?" Vincent questioned. "What about you? Isn't me wanting to hurt them just the excuse you tell yourself because deep down you wanted to kill me? To be rid of me?"

"That's not true."

"Really?" Vincent said, stepping closer. "If you were so scared of me hurting them, you would have killed me long before you tried to."

"You were going to kill them, Vincent. Deep down, you have to know that."

"No."

"Yes!" Scott screamed. "Look at yourself, what you're doing now. Look at Karen." Vincent didn't turn. "You're hurting them, doing what you were always afraid you would do. What I always knew you would do."

"That's not true," Vincent growled, putting his hand around Scott's throat, holding him against the wall. "I never wanted this. You forced me."

"No, I didn't," Scott said, choking.

"Yes, you did!" Vincent screamed, his right hand twitching more violently than ever. "Because of you, Dr. Freeman got rid of me. Because of you, I rotted in your subconscious alone for seven years. Because of you, I came back as this thing, this—this monster."

"You were a monster long before the book made you one. I didn't have a choice. You couldn't see it. Karen couldn't see it. I had to. I had to be there for them, to protect them from you, from what you'd do to them."

"You had to be there?" Vincent asked as he looked at Scott, tears forming in his eyes. "You had to be there!" His right hand twitched wildly as he screamed. "I was there in that cage with you, when you were so broken you didn't even want to escape. I was there afterwards, when you had nightmares of the crows. Where were you when I needed you, Scott?"

Vincent's voice cracked as he spoke. "Where were you when your parents locked me up in your room, every day, for over ten years? Where were you when I scratched at the door until my fingers bled, trying to get out? Where were you when I was starving to death because they wouldn't feed me?"

The anger had left Vincent's eyes, replaced by something else. Replaced by hurt. He could barely speak the words now.

"Where were you when they tried to kill me, to do the procedure themselves? Where were you when I needed help after what happened to April? Did you even try? No, you treated me like everyone else," he screamed, his hand tightening around Scott's throat. Scott saw the look of pure hate in his eyes. "You left me!"

"And you left April!" Scott screamed back.

He regretted it the moment he said it. He was almost afraid to look at Vincent, afraid of what he was going to do. He braced himself for Vincent to kill him, to snap his neck right then and there, but it didn't happen. He looked at his eyes and saw the life go from them. Vincent let go of Scott's throat and backed up, standing silent for a moment before speaking.

"You're right." Vincent's voice sounded broken, in pain. "I left her on that street. I let those men take her." He looked at the floor as tears streamed down his face. "I let them take our daughter." His hand stopped shaking completely.

Scott stayed silent, waiting to see what Vincent would do. He had never seen him so hurt, so broken.

"Maybe I am a monster," Vincent finally said, swallowing the lump in his throat before pointing to Karen. "But she didn't think so." His right hand began to twitch again, but his voice didn't rise. "My entire life, everyone thought I was a mistake, a stray dog that needed to be put down." More tears fell from his face. "But not her. When I met her, for the first time in my life, someone cared. Someone didn't think I was a mistake, just for existing. For the first time, I wasn't alone." His eyes cut up to Scott, the rage returning. "And you took that from me. Took her from me. Left me alone again, for

seven years! Seven years without seeing her face. Seven years without hearing her laugh, or seeing my kids grow up. Seven years without anyone to look at me like I wasn't a monster. Seven years, all alone." Vincent looked down to the floor at Karen, who was waking up. He stepped down to her, putting his hand on her throat.

Scott grabbed the revolver from the floor and pointed it at Vincent, firing it. Misfire. He fired again. And again. Every round misfired.

Scott dropped the gun as he pleaded with Vincent. "Please don't do this. Kill me instead. Don't hurt her."

"I told you, Scott, I'm not going to kill you," Vincent said as he lifted her up, his voice growing cold. "When I was alone, trapped in your head, in your dreams, there wasn't a day that went by that I didn't consider slitting my own throat, ending it. Being free of the pain, of the memories of them. But one thought kept me from it. The thought of showing you what it felt like to be truly alone. How it felt to have everything you love stripped away from you, and then to be left alive, knowing that you'll never see their faces again."

"Please," Karen said, waking up.

"You were wrong," Vincent said to Scott as he lifted Karen in the air, pressing her against the broken window. "I always knew what I was, what I was capable of. There wasn't a moment that passed that I wasn't afraid of hurting them."

Karen fought his grip, her back sliding against the broken glass of the window, as she screamed.

"I told you this was your nightmare," Vincent said as she began to stop fighting. "It was mine too."

Scott heard the sound of Karen's neck crack. Vincent let go, and her lifeless body dropped to the floor. Scott ran over to it, holding her in his arms. He cried as he held her, wiping the blood off her hair.

Vincent walked to the door before turning around to face Scott. He forced himself not to look at Karen. "Tomorrow night. The cemetery." He then stepped out the door and vanished.

Scott sat on the cold floor, holding Karen in his arms. "I'm sorry," he told her as he cried. He rocked her back and forth, looking at her eyes, glazed over, the life taken from them. "I'm so sorry."

Chapter Twenty-Two

Vincent paced the bedroom floor, his head shaking violently. He hated this room but had nowhere else to go. "No, no," he told himself as he walked. He still had Karen's blood on his hands. He tried to wipe it off, but it was stained onto his arm like a brand. Like a reminder.

His hands twitched out of control. It was harder than he'd thought it would be. He tried to stop them from twitching, but he couldn't. All the craving and the longing came back to him all at once, as his head shook like a man possessed.

"No," he whispered to himself. His entire body felt like it was on fire, going to burn up at any second. He could hear his own breathing, the sound of his lungs moving. How could he do this?

He remembered the feeling, the feeling of helplessness he'd felt when April had been taken. The feeling of shame when Karen had found him covered in blood.

Karen. The name caused his head to shake worse, and he fought his hands, fought the twitching, fought the urge. But he couldn't help it. No matter how much he tried not to, he

could feel it now. What it had felt like to put his hand to her throat. To force the life out of her.

Vincent turned sideways to see a crow outside the bedroom window. It had its head tilted sideways, watching him. Judging him. Thinking he was a monster like everyone else.

"Don't look at me," he screamed as he threw a picture frame from the dresser through the window. It crashed into the glass, breaking it, as the crow flew away. But Vincent got worse.

You know what it feels like now, don't you? Vincent's thoughts told him. *You always wanted to know what it felt like, didn't you?*

"Shut up," he screamed, despite no one else being there. "Shut up!" Vincent took the pictures off of the shelves and threw them to the floor. He turned the dresser over on its side, cracking it. He threw the cabinets across the room and ripped off the curtains. But he could still hear the voice inside himself. The craving.

Vincent looked across the room at the mirror on the wall. He saw his reflection in it. A reflection without scars. A reflection without blood. A lie.

"Stop looking at me!" Vincent shouted at his reflection before throwing a kitchen knife through it, cracking the glass. He now looked into it, into his broken reflection, as he backed up to the bedroom door. His legs gave out underneath him, and he slid slowly down the door.

How could he do this? After everything that had happened, how could he kill his family? It wasn't worth it. The look on Karen's face as she'd choked was burned into his memory, and always would be. Vincent began to cry alone

in his bedroom, wanting to stop, but knowing he couldn't. "I didn't mean it."

His head slid down across the door, scraping past the claw marks he had made when he was a boy, trying to get out. Blood started creeping down the walls, consuming the room. Vincent's forearm became warm, but he ignored it. His mind was somewhere else. Where it always was. Thinking of Karen.

"I swear I didn't mean it."

The sun was setting in the sky as Scott buried them. He had dug the first grave for Tommy, on the right side of Joey, and the second for Karen, on the left. He knelt down over her grave. His mouth quivered as he spoke the words he had wanted to for so long but couldn't.

"I'm sorry, for everything. You were right, I shouldn't have killed him. I told myself I was doing it to protect you, but the truth is, I was just scared. I wasn't there when April was taken. I didn't know what to do, how to handle it, so I blamed it on Vincent. I guess I thought if I could protect her from him, then it would make up for not being there." He sighed before continuing. "I know I hurt you. I'm sorry. I should have trusted you, should have trusted him."

The sun was almost down over the horizon, and wind blew through the trees in the backyard. The sound of rustling leaves filled the air as he knelt there.

Tears fell from Scott's eyes as he spoke to his wife. "I have to go now. But I want you to know that I am sorry, for what I did to Vincent, to the kids, to you. It's all my fault. I couldn't protect you, any of you. I was so terrified of what happened to me when I was a kid that I lost what I had now, the most important thing in my life. You."

Scott closed his eyes for a moment, thinking of her.

"I promise," he said, as he looked back down at the grave, "I will protect April. I will save her, whatever it takes." He hesitated. "I will try to save both of them."

The sun set in the sky completely as Scott reached over and put his hand on her grave, feeling the dirt beneath his palm. His voice quivered as he spoke to his wife for the last time. "It's time for me to go. I love you, Karen. I've always loved you."

Chapter Twenty-Three

Scott walked through the graveyard. The full moon was shining in the sky, cutting through the barren twisted limbs of the old oak trees. The light distorted through them, casting wicked shadows on the grass as well as the dirt that covered the graves.

Hundreds of graves, lined up in rows, stretched out as far as Scott could see. Some were old, the grass having long grown over them, but some were fresh, the dirt having just been added, still fresh atop the coffins. Upon each grave sat a tombstone, most made of gray marble. Grass had grown up on the tombstones, vines crawling up it like a spider's web. The tombstones were unique in shape, some small, some arranged in strange twisting patterns. One sat above the rest, shaped like an angel, with wings sprouting out its back and into the air.

Trees were scattered out over the cemetery. Old oak trees, rotted. Their bark fell off to the sides like broken limbs hanging from a corpse, and their branches were long and twisting, cracking as the wind blew them.

The wind was cold, like the night air, but it was calm. Scott felt the chill against his face, but it wasn't overpowering. It moved gently through the brown, rotted grass, forcing the blades to scratch each other like sandpaper.

Scott walked through the graves, passing hundreds as he searched for April. He was carrying nothing save the kitchen knife in his back pocket. He hadn't brought a gun. What was the point? But maybe a knife would change something. Vincent certainly favored them.

But he hoped it wouldn't come to that. He had to get through to Vincent, to save both him and April. He had killed Vincent, made him become this monster. He had to save him. It was what Karen would've wanted.

Scott could hear himself breathe as he walked. He was nervous. What would he say to him? He stepped between the tombstones, feeling the knife move in his pocket. No, it wouldn't come to that. It couldn't.

Scott had been walking for what felt like hours, across the vast cemetery filled with graves and the rotting corpses beneath them, before he saw it—the large oak tree in the center of the cemetery. It was the largest tree in the field, its trunk eight feet across, and its branches stretched up into the sky, twisting into the clouds. From a low-hanging branch, only twenty-five feet in the sky, a chain hung down, black and rusted, its links joining each other in crooked patterns. The chain stretched down from the limb, stopping only ten feet from the ground. From it hung a birdcage, three feet across and five feet tall. Its black bars rounded down from the chain, stretching down to its base. On its side was a door

with rusted hinges. Scott ran as he saw it, the same birdcage that he had been locked in as a child. The same birdcage that still haunted his nightmares. The birdcage that April was now trapped in.

Scott ran to her as fast as he could. He ran past the tombstones stretching off to his sides. He ran past the fallen limbs of the surrounding trees, lying broken on the ground. He ran past the coarse black feathers littered across the grass, as well as an undug grave.

"April," he screamed as he ran to her. The cage hung only a few feet out from the tree, and she saw him.

"Dad?" she screamed.

When Scott was only a few feet away from the cage, Vincent stepped out from behind the tree. "Boo."

Scott stopped in his tracks, almost tripping.

Vincent walked away from it slowly, stopping a dozen feet to the left of the cage. His right hand twitched more violently than before, more than Scott had ever seen it. His eyes seemed hollow, broken.

"Hello, Scott."

"Hey, Vincent," Scott said quietly, as if he was addressing an old friend. "Nice cage."

Vincent was shocked by that but didn't mention it.

"Why this cemetery?" Scott asked.

Vincent looked over the rows of graves for a moment, thinking of the men who had taken April. "This is where I buried them."

Scott nodded, still not showing anger.

"Dad?" April cried from the cage where she sat confined.

Scott held out his hand, motioning for her to be calm. He looked at Vincent, his head twitching as well. He saw the pain in his eyes, the shame on his face. For the first time, Scott realized it. He didn't want this. He had never wanted this.

"Do you really want our daughter in a cage?" Scott asked, his voice calm, almost sympathetic.

Vincent was angered by the sudden attempt at sympathy, by Scott pretending to care now, after everything. "What I wanted was to be with them! To not be alone. But you took that from me!"

"You're right. I did," Scott said, remorseful. "I'm sorry."

Vincent looked at Scott, surprised.

"I took them from you. I told Karen, told myself, that it was because you would hurt them. But that was a lie." Scott stepped closer to Vincent as he spoke. "The truth is, when April was taken, it scared me. I didn't know what to do. Suddenly I was back in that cage, frightened and helpless. I was scared that I couldn't protect her anymore. So I blamed you. I told myself that if I had been there, I could've done something, could've saved her. But I was lying to myself. I would have stood at the window, watching frozen as she was taken, like a coward. But not you," he said, his voice kind as he stepped forward, stopping only a few feet from Vincent. "You tried to save her. Just like you saved me in that cage. Because that's who you are, Vincent. Not this thing, this monster I made you into. I could never see it, but she could." Scott's voice cracked as he took the knife out of his pocket. Vincent stepped back before Scott threw it across the graveyard, it landing by a tombstone. "I'm sorry for what

I did. All of this is my fault. But don't kill April. Don't kill our daughter. Please, Vincent."

Vincent stared at Scott in complete disbelief. It was sincere. He stepped back from him, his mind aching. His breath quickened as his head shook. His head felt like it was on fire as his lungs struggled to move. He hadn't been expecting this, for Scott to apologize.

His head finally stopped twitching, along with his hand. Vincent's craving was gone, Scott could see it in his eyes. Vincent looked up at Scott, the anger, the hate having disappeared from his eyes, replaced by something else. Sadness.

Vincent looked toward Scott, seeing his eyes too. Scott was no longer afraid of him. Vincent looked toward the cage with April sitting in it and then back to Scott. He felt the words catch in his throat as he thought of Karen. "I'm sorry, Scott. But it's too late."

Sccrrreeee

Scott looked up at the sound, seeing the limbs of the tree. He saw thousands of lifeless black eyes watching him from the branches. Hordes of crows sat in the tree, their sharp talons digging into the bark as the sound sliced through the graveyard, echoing through the sky. Their long, distorted wings spread out to each side, twisting unnaturally as they looked down at him. Their necks seemed to be disconnected from their bodies as their heads tilted almost vertically. The moonlight shined thought the missing feathers of their wings, casting a legion of deformed shadows over the ground.

Scott looked over at Vincent, his eyes beginning to water. "Please. Don't do this."

"I'm sorry," Vincent said as the crows cried out, their horrific screech piercing through the night, before taking flight and diving straight down. Straight at April in the cage.

The crows covered the cage, flying around frenzied, almost possessed, as they tore through the bars, clawing at April's skin. Thousands of them seemed to surround her, almost blocking the cage from Scott's view entirely. The sound of their wings beating echoed through the graveyard, almost drowning out her screams. Almost.

"Dad!" she cried out in agony. "Help!"

Scott looked to the cage and the crows that surrounded it, encasing her in a blanket of darkness. He heard his daughter's screams and never hesitated. He walked through the crows, feeling their wretched wings slide over his body as he walked closer to her. He could feel them around him, hear their cries, the flapping of their wings, but still he walked through them.

"Dad!" she cried as she saw him appear amidst the darkness of the crows.

"April," he said back as he stepped toward the cage and grabbed the door. He pulled it, but it wouldn't open. Scott saw the lock. The same lock that had been on his cage so many years ago, but with one difference. There was no keyhole. No way to open it. No escape.

"Dad," she said, taking his hand through the bars.

Scott held it back as he saw her. Her body was littered with cuts from the crows. Blood ran down her side, and the life had already begun to vanish from her eyes. She wouldn't make it much longer.

"Dad, I'm scared," she said.

"I know," he said as he leaned his head against the cage, next to hers. "I am too."

The crows that swarmed them opened up slightly, just enough for Scott to see Vincent watching them. His hand remained still as he looked in, never once twitching.

"Why are you doing this?" Scott screamed at him. "Please! Don't kill her. Not our daughter, not April. Please."

Vincent remained silent, forcing himself not to speak.

"Kill me instead," Scott pleaded with him. "I'm the one who killed you. I did it, not her. She doesn't have to die. Please kill me!" Scott looked at Vincent, begging. "Why won't you just kill me!?"

The words echoed in his head. He fell silent as he realized it all at once. Why Vincent wouldn't kill him. Why he couldn't.

Guardian angel. The words the doctor had said to him after the crash. *You shouldn't have survived. You must've had a guardian angel looking out for you.*

"You can't," Scott said, his eyes widening as he pieced it together. "You aren't connected to April. You're connected to me. That's why you didn't kill me in the crash and take my place. You couldn't. That's why you're killing them instead of me." Scott looked at him with shock. "If I die, you die."

Vincent said nothing as he watched Scott.

Scott looked across the graveyard, at the knife resting in the dirt, as he remembered his promise to Karen. He would protect April. Whatever it took, he would protect her. He looked back at April, taking her hand as crows flew around her. "I love you," he said as he looked into her eyes.

"Dad?"

Scott didn't answer her. He turned and ran across the graveyard, through the crows that surrounded him. He ran to the knife, never hesitating. He had to protect her. He couldn't be afraid. Not this time.

Scott knelt down by the tombstone where the knife rested and picked it up. It was nine inches long, and bright silver. Its metal reflected the moonlight as he gripped the black handle tight. He looked over at Vincent, who stood silently watching him.

Vincent didn't try to stop him.

Scott looked back towards April and smiled at her.

"Dad, don't," she screamed out, seeing what he was about to do.

"It's okay," he told her as he raised the blade up to his chest, tears falling down his face. "I love you." Scott closed his eyes and pushed the blade into his chest, through his heart.

In an instant, the crows vanished, along with the cage April was in. Scott looked sideways, seeing that Vincent had vanished as well. It was over.

April fell to the ground as Scott's legs gave out underneath him. He collided with the dirt as he felt the life slipping out from him. Blood was raining down his chest as she ran over to him.

"Dad," she said as she saw him lying on the dirt. She took him in her arms and raised him up, leaning him against the tombstone behind him. "Dad?" she said again.

Scott coughed as he felt the coldness of the stone hit his back.

"Dad, no," she said, crying as she watched him bleeding out. "You can't leave me."

"It's okay," he said as he looked at her. She was safe now. He had protected her. "It's okay," he reassured her. "You're going to be okay."

"Not without you," she said as she cried.

"You're safe," he said. "That's all that matters."

"Dad," she said once more, but he didn't respond.

Scott looked into her eyes. She was safe. For the first time since he had been taken, he wasn't afraid to die. It didn't matter what happened to him, as long as she was safe. A tear fell down Scott's face as he looked at his daughter for the last time. She looked so much like her mother.

Sccrrreeee

Scott watched in horror as his daughter vanished, replaced by a horde of crows, screeching out as they beat their monstrous wings, scattering into the night sky, revealing Vincent standing behind them.

Scott watched, terrified, as Vincent walked closer to him. "What did you do?"

Vincent stepped up to Scott and knelt down beside him.

"What did you do?"

"It's okay," Vincent said as he looked at Scott with sympathy. "She's okay. They're all okay."

"What?" Scott said. He could barely breathe, much less speak, as he felt himself slipping. Dying.

Vincent looked down at Scott. He deserved the truth. Vincent pointed across the field, at the undug grave that Scott had passed without noticing. "I woke up in that grave seven years ago. After Dr. Freeman did the procedure."

"But"—Scott coughed—"that means—" The words cut off as Scott realized it. "The car crash."

Vincent nodded. "I didn't know how I had come back, only that it wouldn't last. The truth is, I was only back for forty-

five seconds at most. I couldn't stay as long as you were there. So I moved the clock forward, to make you think I had been there longer, and then I cut your brakes and drove off the road before I faded again."

"A coma," Scott said to himself as it sank in.

"Yes," Vincent said.

"Why didn't you just kill me once I was here?" Scott said, coughing up blood. "Why show me the book?"

"One personality can't kill another. Dr. Freeman knew that. I had to get you to do it yourself. There's no book, Scott. There never was. It was to just explain how I was back, and convince you that to protect them from me, you had to kill yourself. I knew if you thought that, you wouldn't hesitate."

Scott looked at Vincent in shock. He didn't look cold, or spiteful. He looked remorseful. "The killings," Scott said. "The hallucinations. Why?"

"I had to keep you distracted. Enough so you wouldn't see the differences, the things I wouldn't know—outside things, voices, that slipped through."

"The crows?" Scott choked.

"They were already here," Vincent said. "They've always been here, in your nightmares. Just like the blood was always in mine."

Scott began to choke as he leaned against the tombstone. "They're alive?"

"Yes," Vincent said, his heart breaking. "They're alive."

Scott looked up at Vincent, not angry but relieved. "Tell Karen I'm sorry." His voice was cracking as he spoke of her. "Tell her I loved her."

"She knows," Vincent said as tears fell from his face. "I'm sorry, Scott, but I had to see them again. I couldn't be alone anymore. I never wanted—"

Scott shook his head, interrupting Vincent. "It's okay."

Vincent nodded back as more tears fell from his face. He stayed by Scott's side as the blood ran from his chest.

Scott felt himself drifting off for the last time. He thought Vincent would be gone, back to his family, but when he looked up, he saw Vincent still kneeling beside him. "What are you still doing here?"

Vincent's swallowed a lump in his throat as he spoke to Scott for the last time. "I didn't want you to be alone."

Scott smiled as he closed his eyes, drifting off. He wasn't afraid anymore.

Chapter Twenty-Four

Vincent woke up. His vision was foggy as he sat up in the hospital bed. He was in a small white room with a heart monitor beside him and a needle sticking in his forearm for the IV drip. As his vision returned to him, he looked to his right and saw April sitting in a chair beside his bed. His eyes watered as he looked at her, the real her, for the first time in seven years. She wore her hair down instead of in a ponytail, and she had more freckles than he remembered, but she still looked perfect to him.

"Dad? You're awake," she said and hugged him before he could react.

"April," he whispered as he felt her embrace. He had almost forgotten what it felt like. He held her back tight as she wept on his shoulder.

"They said you might not wake up," she cried. "I thought I might not see you again."

Vincent let go of her and looked into her eyes. He didn't know what to say. He had thought of this moment for so long, gone over it so many times in his head, but looking at her

now, all the words escaped him. He was home. "I love you," he told her gently.

"I love you too, Dad."

"Dad!" Tommy said as he stepped into the room, May trailing behind him. Tommy rushed up to the bed, hugging him. Vincent looked at him, noticing his voice. He had forgotten how much he sounded like Scott.

Finally, May ran up to the bed and jumped up to the edge of it so she could reach him. She leaned over and hugged him as he looked back at her, shocked. Even though he had known how she would look, how tall she would be, it still almost brought him to tears. She was so big.

"Dad," she said as she held him.

Vincent looked back at all of them, overjoyed. It had been so long.

April saw the look on his face. "What's wrong, Dad?"

She called him Dad. His voice cracked as he spoke. "Nothing."

"May, where'd you go?" Vincent heard a voice say from outside the door. A voice he recognized. He sat forward in the bed and pulled the needle from his forearm, causing a drop of blood to run down it. He got out of the bed and walked to the door as he heard the voice again, coming from down the hall.

"Tommy, where are you?"

Vincent stepped out of the room, seeing Karen at the end of the hallway. Beside her was a stroller that Joey lay asleep in. Vincent was frozen as he looked at her. Saw her jet-black hair, the way it fell down her back. Her brown eyes still glowed to him, and her voice still stopped his heart.

"Scott," she said as she saw him standing there. "You're awake." She ran to him and they embraced each other.

"I thought I'd lost you too," she said as she cried onto his shoulder.

Vincent said nothing as he held her. There was nothing he could say. Nothing that would express how he felt in that moment, embracing his wife again, feeling her touch, hearing her voice. In that moment, any words he tried to say got lost in his mind, and the only thing he could manage was simply her name. "Karen."

She was still crying as she let go, looking at him. "I love you, Scott," she said.

Vincent's eyes cut down at the sound of his name. After everything that had happened, he still cared about Scott, and hearing Karen say his name after what he had done made him scared to look at her.

She saw him look down. "Why are you—" She lost her breath for a moment when she realized. She moved his head back up with her hands and looked into his eyes. "Vincent?"

Vincent looked back into her eyes and saw the same thing he always had. The thing he had seen the first time he had looked at her. The thing that told him everything was okay. That he wasn't alone anymore.

The nightmare was over.

Acknowledgments

I would like to thank my family for all of their support while I was writing this book. Thanks to my mother, the person who first introduced me to the horror genre and encouraged me to write the book. Thanks to my father, who helped me edit the grammar in the first draft. And thanks to my two brothers, who share my love of plot twists, and who helped me pay for the financial aspect of publishing this book. I couldn't have done it without any of you.

Thanks also to MiblArt, who did the cover art and the formatting for this book. I couldn't have asked for a better company to work with. They not only designed an amazing cover but also answered any questions I had about the process, which I really appreciated.

Thanks to my editor, Eliza Dee, who did the editing and proofreading.

Lastly, thank you, for reading this book.

Author Bio

Chad Nicholas is an author who enjoys writing mysteries and thrillers. He also has a love for writing horror novels, despite the fact that he has to watch horror movies in the daytime, like a coward, or else he gets nightmares.

Speaking of Nightmares...

CPSIA information can be obtained
at www.ICGtesting.com
Printed in the USA
LVHW090954051020
667952LV00007B/67/J

9 781734 441642